WORDS OF WARNING

A jagged bolt of lightning cut through the sky beyond the saloon's front window as Clint settled his gaze upon Bittermeyer and said, "I don't much appreciate men who have to knock down weaker folks just so they can feel strong. And even though I only just met you, something tells me that's exactly the type of person you are. And if I've learned anything, it's that you'll pay for the hurt you put on others."

Clint took a few steps backward, keeping his eyes on Bittermeyer and his cronies. Then he turned and walked toward the door. Before he went through, though, he spun on the balls of his feet and let his hand rest on the handle of his Colt.

"This is a nice place you've got here, Bittermeyer," he said. "I just thought you should know that if any of those boys of yours should get any ideas, there's gonna be a whole lot of blood on the floor."

THE GUNSMITH

247

RANDOM GUNFIRE

J. R. ROBERTS

JOVE BOOKS, NEW YORK

RANDOM GUNFIRE

A Jove Book / published by arrangement with
the author

PRINTING HISTORY
Jove edition / July 2002
Copyright © 2002 by Robert J. Randisi.

Visit our website at
www.penguinputnam.com

ISBN: 0-515-13338-8

A JOVE BOOK®
Jove Books are published by The Berkley Publishing Group,
a division of Penguin Putnam Inc.,
375 Hudson Street, New York, New York 10014.
JOVE and the "J" design
are trademarks belonging to Penguin Putnam Inc.

PRINTED IN THE UNITED STATES OF AMERICA

10 9 8 7 6 5 4 3 2 1

ONE

The town of Random, Oklahoma, was very aptly named.

If not for the freak thunderstorm that washed out the trail he'd originally intended to take, Clint Adams wouldn't have ridden anywhere close to the place. But once that strange twist of fate steered him in the proper direction, Clint found himself in the town, which seemed to be filled with suspicious eyes that followed his every move.

Black clouds dumped buckets of water onto Clint's head, making it hard for him to see more than a few feet in any direction and weighing down the Darley Arabian stallion that had been carrying him all the way across the state. When the thunder came, it rolled above him like a train powered by black powder instead of steam. Each bolt of lightning lit up the sky with crackling white fire. And each clap of thunder shook the ground beneath Eclipse's hooves.

To top it all off, the wind tugged at everything that wasn't nailed down, like an invisible hand shaking the stuffing from an old rag doll. Drops of water slapped against Clint's cheek. Every stitch of clothing was plastered against his body. Even breathing was a chore since the raging storm seemed intent on reclaiming every bit of air as its own, no matter if it came from the depth of Clint's lungs.

A gift from the master showman P. T. Barnum, Clint's stallion, Eclipse, was no stranger to performing feats of strength and agility. But the tantrum being thrown by Mother Nature was almost enough to throw Eclipse off all four of his feet. The stallion's progress was slowed to a near crawl as the wet ground sucked every step farther into the mud, causing Eclipse's muscles to strain just to keep moving.

Every time Clint tried to think about which way they were headed, his brain was rattled by another furious explosion from the sky. He knew he wasn't lost, but he also knew that the trail he'd been intending to ride was several miles back and buried beneath a newly created stream. He was still headed north by northeast. At least that much he could be sure about.

If he wanted to figure out much more beyond that, he would have to wait until he could get a clear view of his hand in front of his face. Until then, he kept his head down low and pulled the brim of his hat even further over his eyes to keep the cold, biting rain from spattering against his pupils.

Clint's raincoat felt like a heavy wool blanket that had been wrapped around him like a cocoon. Although made from oiled sailcloth, the coat could only repel so much before it lost the battle against the elements and started pushing down on him like an anchor hanging from the middle of his back. The reins were wrapped so tightly around Clint's left hand that the leather was beginning to bite through flesh. Although he couldn't tell for sure if he was bleeding or not, the pain was starting to get to him after hours of constant gnawing.

But the discomfort served to keep his senses from being dulled by the roaring monotony all around him. Long ago, the rain had started looking like a gray curtain shaking all around him. The water came down so fast that it was impossible to see individual drops. Instead, all Clint could make out was a shifting field of drab, foggy haze against a background that got darker every passing minute. If he didn't find some shelter soon, he knew he would be in a world of trouble.

At first, he thought the sign was just a piece of refuse or even a tree trunk along the side of the trail. But when he got closer, he noticed its large square shape. Another few steps and he could see black, blocky letters painted onto the planks of wood: "NOW ENTERING RANDOM."

There was more on the sign, but Clint wasn't exactly in the mood to read. Lifting his face into the torrential downpour, he tried to catch sight of the town, but only got a face full of water for his troubles. A gust of wind whipped through the air, sucking out Clint's breath before he'd even gotten a chance to take it in.

He suddenly felt as though he was drowning and his heart thumped in reflexive panic. The feeling was gone as quickly as it came, however, and Clint held his hat at an angle so he could take another look.

Sure enough, there was a town in front of him. In fact, the trail had already straightened out into a street with buildings lining it on either side. Another flash of lightning lit up the street, giving Clint a better look at the town he'd entered.

Random flashed before Clint's eyes as the bright, jagged bolt ripped at the seams of the sky. For an instant, he got a better look at the turn of the street and what appeared to be a larger building at the end of the block. In the next moment, however, it was gone, leaving Clint with nothing but a memory to steer by.

With the image fresh in his mind, Clint snapped Eclipse's reins and lowered his face against the storm, which seemed to have picked up even more steam in the last few moments. The Darley Arabian shook its head and snuffed loudly, but plodded on through the water and thick, sucking mud.

"It won't be long now, boy," Clint said while reaching out to stroke the stallion's slippery mane. "Just a little farther and we'll both see about getting ourselves dried off and fed."

Clint doubted that the stallion understood his words, but Eclipse seemed to grasp a bit of their intention. Lowering his own head, Eclipse steeled himself for the last bit of his ride and walked down the rest of the street without so much as a single complaining grunt.

Clint could feel a sniffle itching at the inside of his nose and a sneeze growing at the top of his throat. Rather than worry about just how sick he could get after an entire day of riding in the rain, he took a deep breath, spit out the rain he'd inhaled and tightened the collar of his coat around his neck.

As if sensing that they were about to lose their favorite target, the clouds opened up even further to blacken the sky, allowing the storm to howl around Clint's ears like a ravenous animal.

TWO

Crawling in the darkness like a predator closing in on its prey, the lean figure kept quiet and still until another crack of lightning sent a flashing pulse of light through the luxurious room he'd rented. Stark white light snapped through the tidy space, reflecting off polished mirrors as well as a set of dirty silver platters which bore the weight of an unfinished evening meal.

The man smiled to himself while stretching out to grab hold of the edges of his soft feather mattress. Beneath him, a young girl lay naked on top of the sheets; her hands reaching out for him while her eyes darted nervously from one shadow to the next.

He watched her try to hide her nervousness and was amused with the way she glanced toward the window like a scared child who still thought that every storm was filled with monsters aching to carry her away.

"What's the matter, Belle?" he asked. "Afraid of a little thunder?"

Lifting her hands toward the man's bare chest, she ran her fingers along his muscles and shifted her body like a fidgeting cat. "That storm's getting awful close, is all. The noise makes me jump sometimes."

Leaning down so that his lips were brushing against her ear, the man said, "Well I'm a whole lot closer. Maybe you should be more afraid of me."

For a moment, there was a trace of genuine fear in the girl's eyes. Even in the darkness, the emotion could be seen like a flicker of light, similar to the bigger ones crossing between the black clouds outside. She looked up at him for that moment and was finally able to force a smile onto her face.

"You're just trying to give me a fright," she said. Her young body was somewhat plump, but all the curves were in the proper places. Her hips were smooth and round, as was her finely contoured backside. When she got ahold of the man's shoulders, she pulled him down on top of her, pressing her large, firm breasts against him in a way that made the rod between his legs grow stiff against her crotch.

Looking down at her, the man took in the sight of her high cheekbones and the way her brassy blond hair caught the light of the room's single candle and turned it into a warm, golden glow. His hands moved down her side, tracing the line of her body all the way down and back up again. His fingers savored the creamy perfection of her flesh as his thumb glanced across the delicate firmness of her erect nipple.

"Maybe I do take a bit of pleasure from seeing you get scared," he said. "Just a little anyway."

Her lips formed into a well-practiced pout. "Why would you want to do something like that?"

Moving his hand down over her breast and onto her stomach, he let his tongue flick out and take a brief taste of her fragrant neck. "I like the way it makes you squirm." Slipping his hand even lower, he held his finger over the swollen nub of her clitoris and added, "You groan just a little when you're surprised. Your eyes close up and you take in a quick little breath. It's quite a sight to see."

The girl had been doing just that as soon as she felt his hands on her most sensitive area. Her hand reflexively went down to his, but stopped when he began making small, fast circles that sent shudders of pure ecstasy rippling through her body. Her pussy was getting so wet that she could feel the juices trickling down the inside of her thigh. The man let his fingers slide down her vagina, then slipped two easily inside.

Her breath caught in the back of her throat and her spine arched against the mattress. "Oh yes," she groaned. "Deeper."

The man kept his eyes on her face. His smile widened as one hand closed around her breast while the other pumped between her legs. He kept his strokes shallow for the moment, savoring the way her expression became fitful and tortured the longer she was denied what she craved so much.

First, his fingers slid just a little further inside of her. Then, as he felt her start to buck and grind her hips against him, he took his hand away and brought it up to her mouth.

The girl instinctively opened her lips and allowed him to touch her tongue. She knew what he was doing and allowed the corners of her mouth to turn up in a dirty little smile. "I'd rather taste you," she whispered.

"Is that so?" Moving down along her body, the man slid over her skin until his face settled between her legs. "You'll just have to wait a little longer."

THREE

She started to say something, but the words caught in the back of the girl's throat. A stifled moan fought to escape her mouth, but couldn't get free as she felt the man's lips press against her vagina and his tongue penetrate her creamy depths.

Unable to do much more than squirm on the bed, she grabbed a handful of the man's short black hair, pulling his face even deeper between her legs while she locked her ankles around the middle of his back. Bucking against him like an animal, she grit her teeth and cried out as another wave of thunder shook the ceiling over their bed.

The man could feel her skin twitching between his lips. Every spot he touched with his tongue quivered in time to the girl's racing breaths. Unable to control himself any longer, he raised himself up and crawled toward the headboard. Once he was in the right position, he mounted her and thrust his cock deep inside the girl's waiting body.

Upon penetrating her, he only allowed himself to stay inside for a moment before pulling out again. The next time, he only let the tip of his penis enter her, keeping it there as the girl bucked her hips hungrily against his body.

"Don't make me wait," she moaned. "I want it hard! I want it *now*!"

Her cries were better than music to the man's ears. Just hearing them caused his rod to become even harder. The girl's pussy clenched around him and she started to rake her nails down his back in an attempt to pull him deeper inside.

The thrust of his hips caused them both to grunt with animal pleasure. Every time he pushed his hips forward, the man clenched his teeth and strained his muscles, savoring the feeling of completely dominating the girl beneath him.

When she tried to cry out again, her voice became a muffled groan as a hand clamped down hard against her mouth. Feeling that, the girl opened her eyes and found herself staring into the leering face of her lover. His expression was almost enough to send another, more powerful, jolt of fear throughout her body.

Removing his hand, the man thrust into her again while sliding his fingers through her golden hair. "You like that, girl?" he hissed. "You like that, don't you."

Her first impulse was to shake her head, struggle, get away, but that only lasted for another split second, until the entire length of his hard cock was buried between her legs, its tip rubbing against a spot inside of her that sent the first glimpses of orgasm down the muscles of her legs and up the column of her spine.

"Yes," she whispered. "God, yes."

The man raised up on his elbows like a snake getting ready to sink its fangs into the girl's tender flesh. Their sweating bodies slapped together as he thrust harder and harder into her, rocking the bed against the wall every with every stroke.

Her eyes clamped shut once again, the girl dug her nails into the man's shoulders and wrapped her legs tightly around him. She pumped her hips in time to his rhythm, quickening her pace as they both raced toward climax.

Finally, the man buried his cock deep inside of her and arched his back as his explosive release sent waves of pleasure through every muscle of his body.

The girl's hand went instinctively to her clitoris, pressing down on the swollen nub of flesh as her own orgasm pumped wildly through her system once again. She was so wet that her fingers were glistening in the dim light when she brought them back.

Seeing this, the man grabbed her by the wrist, lifted her hand to his mouth and ran her fingertips along his bottom lip. Her moisture had the musky flavor of her sex and the consistency of fresh honey. When he licked it off of her, he noticed the girl smiling widely, her eyes glimmering with renewed desire.

Even though her body was still weak from the passion that was still burning inside like an ember, she sat up and tried to get as much of her body pushed against him as she could. She brushed her leg along his side and pressed her breasts against his chest. The more she touched him, the more she wanted to feel him inside her again. Already, expectant tingles surged through her thighs.

"Can I taste you now?" she asked.

The man rolled onto his side and propped one leg up, allowing her hand to reach for his shaft. After a few gentle strokes, his body was responding to her touch. He didn't have to say a word to get her to do exactly as he wanted. It was as though he could feel the spell that he'd woven around her like some kind of web that drew her in to the exact spot he'd kept open just for her.

Lowering her head as she moved down his chest, she let her hair dangle over his skin, brushing over him while she slowly eased her face between his legs. With her hair still spread out on his stomach and hips, she opened her mouth and closed her lips around the head of his cock, swirling her tongue in languid circles.

For the next few moments, the man leaned back and enjoyed the sensation of her mouth gliding over his hard shaft. More than once, she took him all the way into her mouth while sucking on him like a piece of thick candy.

He slipped his hands through her hair, playing with the silken strands and savoring the touch of them between his fingers.

When she brought her head up, the girl lifted her eyes so she could look at him while smiling broadly. The tip of her tongue peeked out from between her lips to run along the bottom of his penis. "Are you ready so soon?" she asked hopefully.

Nodding, the man said, "Oh yes. I'm more than ready."

FOUR

The girl climbed on top of him and lifted her hips before settling over his cock. Spreading her legs wide, she lowered herself down until she impaled herself on his thick column of flesh. She let out a contented moan and closed her eyes as she took every inch of him inside.

"I've got a surprise for you," he said in a mischievous whisper.

"Should I open my eyes?"

After shifting beneath her, the man's voice drifted through the air in a calm spot between bursts of thunder that still raged outside. "All right. You can look now."

Not quite sure what to expect, the girl lifted her hands to her face and then parted them with a flourish. All traces of joy in her expression dropped away the moment she caught sight of the smooth, curved blade being held less than an inch away from her face.

He gripped the knife in a bony fist, savoring the way her muscles tightened in response to the sight of it. Still thrusting inside of her, he touched the edge of the blade to her throat just to see what she would do.

Too scared to move, the girl froze. Her eyes were white as saucers in the dark as they strained to see exactly where the blade was moving next on her body. She'd been told about this man and how strange he sometimes acted, but those stories had only made her try to be around him even more. The thought of bedding such a man made her tremble, and until this moment, she'd thought this one had been worth the wait.

"What are you—"

"No," he said, cutting her off with a bit of pressure on the knife. "Don't say anything."

Reaching up to press his finger to her lips, the man silenced her as he would a child, shushing her quietly as the rain beat against the windowpane.

"I've got one question for you," he said. "And be sure to think before you answer."

The girl's chin moved slightly, but stopped when she felt just how close the knife was to her throat.

Sliding out from beneath her, the man kept the blade in place while leaning up closer to her ear. "Who do you belong to?" he asked.

Now confusion mixed in with the fear in her eyes, twisting her face into a bizarre mask. When she spoke, her voice could barely be heard over the steady patter of rain on the roof. Each word was carefully formed in an effort to keep her jaw from moving any more than was necessary. "I . . . I don't understand."

"Yes or no," he whispered. "You don't have time to think it over."

The girl blinked a couple of times, wondering if this was really happening or possibly some kind of cruel joke. When she felt the knife's edge break her skin just enough to start a trickle of blood down her neck, she drew in a sharp breath, closed her eyes . . . and prayed.

After a few moments had passed, the man spoke again. His voice was quiet. Calm. "You'd best answer me. I'm known for a lot of things, but patience sure isn't one of them. I'll give you one more second."

That second came and went.

"Now," he whispered. "Who do you belong to?"

A single tear pushed out from the corner of her eye. "Y . . . you," she stammered. "I belong to you."

"That's right."

The blade pressed a little harder against her skin, widening the slender rip in her flesh by a fraction of an inch.

Suddenly, his hand moved in a blur of motion, carrying the blade in a tight arc away from the girl's throat. The weapon left his grasp and whipped through the air, turning one complete circle before slamming into the thick wood of the door's frame.

"I had a lovely time, darling," he said while hopping off the bed and walking toward the rumpled pile of clothing on the floor. "You did a splendid job."

For a moment, the girl stayed in the same position as if she'd been frozen there by a wave of ice. Her eyes blinked once and then she fell onto her side while clutching at the dripping wound at her throat. It was all she could do to lie there quietly, fighting back the impulse to cry out or say something to the man, who got dressed as though nothing out of the ordinary had happened.

Seconds ticked by and the girl wondered if she might be dying. Although there wasn't much blood on her hands, she was starting to feel weak and dizzy. That feeling subsided, however, the moment the man had finished putting on his clothes and opened the door.

"I take care of my possessions, darling," he said with a tip of his hat. "And as of this moment, you're one of my treasures."

He stepped outside and slammed the door behind him. Only then did the girl allow herself to take a full breath.

FIVE

The building Clint had seen appeared to be a saloon, but he couldn't tell for sure. There were a few letters stenciled onto the front window, but they'd been washed away in a previous storm. Just as he was about to run into the large building, he spotted a pair of open barn doors beckoning to him from the other side of the street like a giant, gaping smile that was two front teeth short of a full set.

Steering toward those doors, Clint was relieved to see a beefy figure waddle out into the rain, holding up a lantern to guide his way. Coming in from the storm, Clint felt a moment of shock as the rain suddenly stopped pelting the top of his head and his eyes could take in everything around him without straining or being stung by cold droplets of water.

"Helluva night out there, huh?" the barrel-chested man hollered while pulling shut the barn doors.

Clint couldn't answer right away. Instead, he was too busy sliding off of Eclipse's back and shaking the water from his coat. He entertained the thought of peeling the coat from his back, but remembered that he'd only have to run outside in a few minutes anyway.

15

Once the doors banged shut, the sounds of the storm were instantly muffled. The rain was more of a looming presence than a constant assault, and while the thunder still sounded like cannon fire, they were at least distant cannons instead of guns blasting directly into Clint's ears.

Plucking the hat from his head, Clint ran a hand through his hair and felt the runoff coursing down his back. He wiped the water from his eyes and took a look at the man who stood in front of him.

A couple inches shorter than Clint, the stocky gentleman shook his head and used the back of his sleeve to wipe away some of the water that dripped from his full, bushy beard. His cheeks were flushed and his lips parted in a wide, gap-toothed smile. "Howdy, mister," he said in a robust tone. "I said it's a helluva night."

"You sure did," Clint said while taking in his surroundings. "And it's just as true now as the first time you said it." He was in a barn with a row of three stalls built along one wall. The rest of the space was filled with various tools, a battered coach and several bales of hay. A loft hung precariously overhead from rotten beams. Every clap of thunder shook a few blades of straw loose which fluttered down to the dirty floor.

The stout man walked over to Eclipse and took hold of the reins. "Don't blame ya for bein' cross. You look like you've been drowned and washed up on a muddy shore." Wincing slightly, he added, "No offense meant."

Clint looked down at himself. "I'd be offended if it wasn't true. Actually, I feel just a little worse than I look."

The other man whistled softly. "Then I'll bet you could use a drink."

"That would be a pretty safe bet," Clint replied. "Is that the saloon I passed on my way over here?"

"The big place at the other end of the street? That'd be one of 'em. You head on over there and they'll set you up real nice. Tell 'em I sent ya and they might even give you a discount on a room. I, uh, take it you'll be sticking around for a bit."

"Yeah. In fact, I was kicking around the idea of sleeping in the stall next to my horse rather than go back out into that rain. But then again, a man can only get so wet before it just doesn't matter anymore."

"That's the spirit." The stocky man reached out to slap Clint on the shoulder. He then held out the same hand and waited until it was received by his guest. "The name's Harrold. I own this stable and can get you just about anything you need around here. If I can't get my hands on it," he added with a wink, "I know who can."

"I appreciate the concern, Harrold, but I think a hot meal and some coffee should do me just fine for now. I'm Clint, by the way."

"Well, Clint, if'n you change your mind, you know where to find me. I'll be sure to tend to this animal of yours jus' like it was my own."

Looking over to the Darley Arabian, Clint noticed that Eclipse was already dozing off. He pat the stallion on the muzzle and hefted the saddlebags over his shoulder. Harrold was already busying himself with removing the saddle and fetching a dry blanket to keep the horse from catching too much of a chill.

Too tired to even think about the liveryman's fee, Clint gave Harrold a parting wave and buttoned his coat all the way back up to his neck. He stepped back outside into the rain while pulling his hat down low over his eyes. Although the storm was letting up somewhat, the rain still felt like a downpour compared to the short time he'd spent indoors.

But rather than think about the rivers going down his back or the puddles in his boots, Clint focused on the warm glow of the saloon's windows down the street. He thought about how great it would be to get something hot in his belly, and by the time his stomach started growling loud enough to drown out the sound of raindrops slapping against his hat, he was stepping up to the saloon's front door.

An explosive burst of thunder sounded just as Clint was walking inside. The sound reminded him of someone shooting at his heels with both barrels of a shotgun. The moment he came in from the storm, he could feel the heat emanating from a huge, roaring fireplace that took up a good portion of the middle of the room. Flames crackled from a large square structure that resembled an oversized forge with a chimney coming straight down from the ceiling.

The place actually looked bigger on the inside than it did on the outside since the building itself was much longer than it was wide. A massive bar carved from thick, chipped oak ran down the length of one of the longer walls to curve around a back corner and continue for about ten more feet in the rear. Only two bartenders patrolled the rows of taps and shelves of bottles, which was more than enough since there were no more than a dozen or so patrons inside.

A small stage sat dormant on the other side of the room next to a lonely piano. The rest of the room was taken up by tables used for eating and gambling, most of which were empty. There was a set of stairs at either end of the room that, according to a brightly painted sign, led to rooms available for rent.

Before he even realized his feet were moving, Clint found himself standing next to the huge fireplace. He held his hands palms out toward the flames after unbuttoning his coat and shaking off the excess water.

Although he heard the footsteps coming his way, Clint didn't bother looking for their source until he knew it was right beside him. He turned to look just as a small hand tapped him on the shoulder.

"You look like hell, mister," an attractive redhead said. She looked up at Clint with intelligent green eyes. Her hair came down just past her shoulders and seemed to soak in the firelight, which blended in seamlessly with the amber streaks running throughout. Full, succulent lips curled into a wry grin as she pulled her hand back and wiped it on the white apron tied around her waist. A simple peasant shirt clung to her trim body and a plain dark skirt hung from small, rounded hips.

Clint shook his head as though he was clearing out some cobwebs once he realized he'd spent the last second or two staring at the girl who'd approached him. "I look like hell, huh? Well, that seems to be the general consensus."

Removing a small bar towel that had been hanging from her apron strings, the redhead dabbed at Clint's cheeks. "There you go. That's a little better," she said before placing the towel in his hand. "I'm Lucy. Can I get you something to warm you up?"

"Actually, Lucy, that's exactly what I was hoping for."

SIX

Sitting at the table closest to the fireplace he could get, Clint felt as though the crackling flames were the sun's rays on his back. Heat from the snapping logs washed over him and started making him feel less like a drowned dog and more like a regular human being. Once his skin was no longer puckering from the constant dampness beneath his clothes, he allowed himself to kick back and truly relax.

"You feeling any better?" Lucy asked as she brought over another steaming cup of coffee along with a bowl of hot beef stew.

Clint took the stew from her and held the bowl in his hands for a few moments to relish the warmth through the wood. He set it down the moment the delicious aroma got to his nose and nearly started shoveling in the food before the server handed him his spoon.

" 'Better' doesn't quite cover it," Clint said. "I feel like a new man. And thank you for asking."

"Well, you sure look a lot better. Where did you ride in from, anyway?"

"Texas," Clint replied between bites. "Rode up into Oklahoma a while ago and have been working my way through ever since." He paused to fill his mouth again and savor the taste before continuing. "I thought I might head toward Bartlesville or Ponca City."

Standing with her hips cocked to one side, Lucy grasped her empty tray in both arms. "Most folks tend to know where they're going before they get there. But I guess that's too much trouble sometimes."

Clint gave a quick laugh and shrugged. "You know something? Sometimes, that *is* a little too much trouble. That kind of planning tends to take the fun right out of travel, don't you think?"

"It's been a long time since I've gone much of anywhere. Way too long."

Already, the stew was almost gone and Clint took a moment to work on his coffee before it had a chance to cool off. "You don't strike me as the homebody type."

"Oh really?" Lucy said with a wide grin. "And what makes you say that?"

"I don't know. Something about the eyes, maybe." Clint took that opportunity to let his own eyes wander over the redhead's figure.

Her skin was smooth and flawless in the firelight, giving off a glow that was enhanced by the dancing flames. The curves of her body flowed invitingly beneath her clothing. As she turned around to check on another customer, the tight lines of her backside were outlined by her loose-fitting skirt. The shadows played off of her body to highlight the way her hips twitched when she walked away, as well as the supple bounce of her breasts as she returned.

"Can I get you anything else?" she said once she'd come back to stand at Clint's table.

"I can think of several things."

"How about something from the bar or kitchen?"

Grinning, Clint shook his head. "In that case, no. I think I'll just sit here for a bit and enjoy not being wet for a while." The rain was still a constant presence from outside. It beat against the roof in a never-ending rhythm like impatient fingers on a desktop. "Is there somewhere close that I can stay for the night?"

"Is upstairs close enough?"

"Only if the rooms aren't solely for drunks who can't see past their own noses and smell worse than a soggy mattress."

Lucy's lips curved into a full, rose-hued smile. "They're worth the price. In fact, the owner of the place stays here, if that tells you much of anything. In fact, I wouldn't mind sleeping there myself."

Standing up, Clint fished some money from his pocket and slipped it into Lucy's apron. "I'll keep that in mind. When you get some free time, why don't you come back and we can continue our discussion?"

"If you don't mind waiting."

"It looks like I'm not going anywhere."

"Then that sounds fine. I should be done in about—"

Just then, a sound rumbled overhead that was almost loud enough to be mistaken for thunder. The only difference was that thunder didn't work its way over the ceiling before clomping down the stairs. Also, thunder didn't come from a tall, lean man dressed in a rumpled black suit and grinning like a cat who'd just swallowed its first canary.

The man walked in a way that purposely drew attention to himself. He then put on the air of ignoring the looks he'd been trying so very hard to get from everyone in the saloon. When he made his way down the middle of the staircase closest to the bar, he stopped and buttoned his black suit jacket.

Looking up to the sound of rolling thunder, he grinned and said, "Hell of a night, eh, Jones?"

"Yessir, Mr. Bittermeyer," one of the bartenders replied.

SEVEN

The man on the stairs turned his gaze immediately toward Lucy. As soon as he found the redhead, his eyes narrowed and he continued his descent. "There you are, Lucy! How about you warm me up just the way I like it? And while you're at it . . . get me something to drink, as well."

Keeping her back to the stairs, Lucy rolled her eyes so Clint could see the exasperated look on her face. "Sorry, but I've got to go," she whispered.

"I'll wait."

Clint watched as the man everyone called Mr. Bittermeyer came walking down the stairs and strutted around the place as though he owned everything in it. It didn't take long before Clint realized that this man in fact *did* own the saloon. Unfortunately, he treated the workers and customers alike as though they'd been bought and paid for along with the four walls and huge fireplace.

After Bittermeyer settled down at a seat near the end of the bar, Clint noticed someone else walking down the same set of stairs. This new arrival didn't have a fraction of the ceremony that Bittermeyer had put into his own entrance. In fact, the woman who came down to the main room kept her head down low and averted her eyes when

Clint looked in her direction. She let one hand hang casually at her side while the other remained up near her neck.

Clint's curiosity turned into something much more serious when he saw the trickle of blood coming from beneath the hand covering the woman's neck. Getting to his feet, Clint made his way to the foot of the stairs just as the woman came off the final step.

"Excuse me," he said.

Clint didn't get the chance to say anything else before the woman turned away from him and started walking quickly to one of the doors at the back of the room. His hand flashed out to take hold of her by the elbow. Although he was careful not to hurt the woman, he was also certainly not about to let her get any farther.

"I'm sorry, ma'am, but I don't think you heard me," Clint said with subtle conviction in his voice.

She still wouldn't look at him. Instead, she turned her face away and tried to cover herself even more. When she pressed her hand against her neck, the blood seeped out between her fingers. "I heard you," she whispered. "Just let me go."

Once Clint saw that she wasn't trying to pull away from him any longer, he let up on his grip while still keeping her in place. "You look like you're hurt. If something frightened you, perhaps I can help." Leaning in closer, he asked softly, "Who did this to you?"

Slowly, she looked up at him. Wispy blond hair hung in curls around her face and the woman's deep blue eyes were starting to fill with tears. She had the kind of innate beauty that made men want to run to her rescue and take care of whatever it might be that was stealing the smile from her face. Even though Clint knew better than to believe everything that came out of a pretty face, he was also still a man and had all the innate weaknesses men were born with.

"If whoever hurt you is still here," Clint said, "I can make sure you at least get home safely."

For the briefest of moments, the woman's face brightened up and she moved her hand away from her neck to dry one of her eyes. With that subtle gesture, she showed Clint the shallow cut across her throat. And when she saw the look in his eyes, she immediately placed her hand back over the wound.

"It looks a lot worse than it is," she insisted. "I should just leave now."

"You still here, Belle?" came a booming voice from the other end of the saloon. "Why don't you go home and get some rest." Looking around to the small group of locals who'd gathered around him, Bittermeyer added, "You're going to need it."

The men near Bittermeyer turned to take a long, leering look at the blonde and started laughing with dirty smiles plastered across their faces. Bittermeyer himself stood up tall and proud as though he'd just given the performance of a lifetime. In fact, he seemed to be about one second away from taking a bow.

Clint moved his hand over the blonde's arm until it was resting on her shoulder. He turned to her and pretended as though he was taking a look around the room. "You don't have to say anything," he said quietly. "Just nod if that's the man that did this to you."

Her first impulse was to turn away. But then she caught sight of something in another part of the room that caused her to take a deep breath and pull herself up straight. She locked eyes with Clint for less than a second, nodded once and walked away.

Looking for the source of the blonde's momentary strength, Clint found Lucy staring intently toward the staircase; the muscles in her face and arms twitching as though it took all she had to keep from running to the blonde's side.

Clint had seen more than enough.

Turning toward the bar, he walked along its length until he was on the outer edge of the men circling Bittermeyer. Every one of those locals hung on Bittermeyer's words as if they were the only thing keeping them up. When he stopped talking, they all nodded. And when he stared into Clint's eyes, they all turned around like a loyal pack of guard dogs.

"You're not from here, are you?" Bittermeyer asked.

"Actually, no," Clint replied. "And I was just starting to like this place. Especially the peace and quiet."

"You'll have to forgive me if I'm a little boisterous, but I have had a very . . . eventful evening." At that last part, Bittermeyer's audience broke into raucous laughter.

"Oh, I understand. And no evening would be complete without a stiff drink and the blood of a woman on your hands."

Instead of looking offended, Bittermeyer only cocked his eyebrows and took a pull from the glass of whiskey that had been placed on the bar in front of him. Some of the men around him were starting to look a little confused. The rest were slowly drawing closer to where Clint was standing.

"I could have you thrown out of here," Bittermeyer said plainly. "Or worse."

Clint didn't bat an eye. "And if you cut a woman's throat for sport, I could have you arrested." The corner of his mouth turned up in a steely grin. "Or worse."

EIGHT

The air crackled with so much tension that even the thunder outside didn't seem quite as loud as it had a few moments ago. For the next few moments, Bittermeyer sized up Clint with eyes that were the color of petrified wood. They looked as though they'd been alive and vital at one time, but had hardened into impenetrable stone long ago. Those eyes burned with the cold intensity of genuine cruelty.

Staring into those eyes, Clint was certain that the girl had steered him in the right direction. Bittermeyer not only looked like the kind who would take a knife to a woman, but he looked like the type who was capable of much, much more . . . and much, much worse.

Bittermeyer's intensity burned away like fog in front of the sun, to be replaced by a look of genuine amusement. "You certainly could arrest me," he said. "But there's one problem. You see . . . there's no law in Random."

Clint took a deep breath and scanned the faces in the saloon. Every one of them was turned in his direction, so it didn't take much to get a feel for them all. Although he didn't think any of the locals would present much of a problem in a fight, he still didn't want to hurt anyone based on a gut-level dislike for the man in the rumpled black suit.

Squaring his shoulders and allowing his top lip to curl into a sneer, Bittermeyer said, "There's one more problem. I own this saloon. And since I don't much appreciate being accused of such vile acts as what you've been talking about, I'd appreciate it if you got the hell out of my saloon before something tragic happens to you."

Clint put on his own steely expression and took a slow step toward the bar. Every one of the other men except for Bittermeyer took a reflexive step away. The mean expressions on their faces had about as much real grit behind them as a club made out of balsa wood.

Turning to glance over his shoulder, Clint noticed that the blond woman was still standing near the front door of the saloon. Next to her, Lucy was tending to the wounds on her neck with what appeared to be a wet rag. As he turned to look back at Bittermeyer, Clint made sure to meet the gaze of every one of the other men, if only for a split second.

A jagged bolt of lightning cut through the sky beyond the saloon's front window as Clint settled his gaze upon Bittermeyer. "You know something?" he asked. "I don't much appreciate men who have to knock down weaker folks just so they can feel strong. And even though I may have just met you, something tells me that that's exactly the type of person you are. If I've learned anything, it's that you'll pay for the hurt you put on everyone else. That's not a law you'll find in any book or any court. That's the law of the world." Clint took a few steps backward, making sure to keep his eyes on Bittermeyer as well as his group of followers. After a few seconds ticked by, he turned and started walking for the door, every one of his senses on the alert for any sign of an attack.

For the moment, Bittermeyer's dogs seemed more than content to stay right where they were. Before he got to the door, Clint spun on the balls of his feet and let his hand rest on the handle of the modified Colt at his side.

"This is a nice place you've got here, Bittermeyer," he said. "I just thought I'd let you know there's going to be a whole lot more blood on your floors if any of those boys around you decide to get a wild hair."

Bittermeyer set his glass on the bar and shoved aside the men standing in his way. Stepping out in front of the small group, he set both hands on his hips and put on a hurt expression. Besides that, the gesture also displayed the Smith & Wesson revolver with the engraved silver handle hanging in a shoulder holster beneath his jacket.

"Did I do something to offend you, sir?" Bittermeyer asked.

Clint looked behind him to where Lucy and the blonde were still standing. Playing back everything he'd seen in his mind, he held the door open and signaled for the blonde to leave. "I'll let you know," he said, and then followed her out into the pouring rain.

"Why did you do that?"

The question hung like steam from the blonde's mouth until it was quickly washed away by the rain. She stood in the doorway of a building across the street, huddled there beneath the narrow eave with her collar pulled up around her neck.

Once Clint ran over to her, she repeated the question while stomping on the porch angrily. "Why would you do something like that? I don't even know who you are!"

Clint let her scream until she sapped her energy. It didn't take long, and soon the woman was leaning against the door with her arms folded across her chest. Once she'd calmed down, she relaxed enough to allow Clint to see the wound on her throat. Between Lucy's cleansing with the towel and the continuous flow of rain, most of the blood had been washed away, leaving nothing more than a thin red line.

Reaching out to touch his finger to her throat, Clint said, "That doesn't look so bad."

"No," the blonde replied while slapping away his hand with the back of her wrist, "it's not. But you had to get Mr. Bittermeyer all rattled anyhow."

"Did he cut you on accident?"

She paused for a second, staring at Clint with a mixture of rage and embarrassment. "No," she finally said.

"Then I don't feel bad about what I did. By the way, I didn't do much of anything besides put a little scare into him. He probably won't come near you for a while."

"He doesn't scare, mister. Believe me, I know."

"Then that's all the more reason for you to get away from him. Maybe even get away from this town if you have to. Whatever led up to that," Clint said while pointing to the wound, "it can't be anything good. If you stay around that man in there, it'll only get worse."

The rain was still coming down in buckets, but Clint barely noticed it. Partly because of the woman huddling in the shadows in front of him, and partly because a part of him still hadn't dried off from the last soaking he'd endured.

"You never answered my question," she said after a while. "Why did you do that for me?"

This time, there was no anger in her voice. No accusation. Just simple curiosity.

Shrugging, Clint said, "I don't know. Could have been a lot of things. I couldn't just stand by and let that man brag to his friends about what he'd done to you. When I saw you come down those stairs, I saw the way you looked at him and the way you carried yourself and I knew you weren't in good shape. You looked like you needed help."

For the first time since he'd laid eyes on her, the blond woman looked at Clint . . . and smiled. "How could you tell all that just by looking at me?"

"Just a knack I have. It gets me into a lot of trouble."

They both laughed at that and then suddenly realized they were still out in the middle of a storm.

"You're soaking wet," she said. "Since you saved me from having to go home with Mr. Bittermeyer, why don't you come home with me? You can get some rest and a change of clothes. It's the least I can do."

Clint enjoyed the light that was creeping back into the blonde's eyes. He could see her spirits rising as though a shadow was being peeled away from her face. He had a strange suspicion that she would need to be watched for the rest of the night, just in case this Bittermeyer person tried to reclaim what he thought was his. But rather than bring the shadows back to the woman's face, Clint kept his smile where it was and placed his coat on her shoulders.

"I'd appreciate that," he said. "I'd appreciate that very much indeed."

NINE

Alonzo Bittermeyer stood at his bar and took another drink of his whiskey. He held up his glass and gazed at the smooth brown liquid through the light of his lanterns. After he downed the expensive liquor, he pitched the glass onto his floor and watched his men jump.

"Clean that up!" Bittermeyer screamed.

The younger of the two barkeeps raced for a broom that was propped up in the corner and got busy sweeping the broken shards into a pile and then into a small tin dustpan. He knew better than to look at Bittermeyer until he was done with his appointed task. Meeting the other man's eyes any sooner would have just made him angrier.

Wheeling around to look at the group of locals who'd circled around him, Bittermeyer spoke in a voice that started off as a rumble and built up into a bellowing roar. "Could somebody tell me just who . . . the hell . . . was that?"

There wasn't a single man among the group of Bittermeyer's followers that seemed ready or willing to answer that question. Instead, they all turned their eyes in another direction and did their best to pretend they hadn't even heard it. Most of them looked as though they would rather weather the storm outside than the one brewing right in front of them.

Bittermeyer was used to such behavior in the men. In fact most of the time he even encouraged it. But now, seeing the cowed look on their faces and the subservient stoop in their spines only made him angrier that none of them would give him what he wanted.

Slamming his fist on the bar once again, Bittermeyer lunged toward the older barkeep. "Then you answer me, Jones! Who in the bleeding hell was that?"

Jones shrugged slightly and shook his head. He might have been around too long to be scared as easily as the others in the saloon, but he wasn't stupid enough to show it. "I never seen him before," he said. "Must be new in town."

"Well, isn't that convenient?" Bittermeyer said. "He thinks he can just strut in here and talk to me like I'm nothing but some punk kid who had too much to drink!" His voice calmed down in the space of a heartbeat when he added, "And after I just had such a nice night breaking in that new girl working this place."

The locals around him grinned, but still seemed too nervous to laugh outright.

Glancing around like a wolf scanning the forest for a lame deer, Bittermeyer searched the saloon with his eyes as the rage seeped back into his face. "Where'd Lucy go? I'll be damned if I'm going to lose her to that pompous son of a bitch along with Belle! You boys," he said while pointing to the locals gathered around him, "go find that smart-mouthed ass and explain to him why he should mind his manners when he's in my establishment. And if you see either of them two women out there, bring them back to me where they belong."

The group seemed happy to have any excuse to leave the saloon. That, added to the fact that they were allowed to walk the streets of Random without having to answer

to another soul, made them even more anxious to carry
out their appointed task.

   After downing their drinks to stoke the fires of courage
in their bellies, the locals filed through the door and
walked out of the saloon.

   Bittermeyer watched them leave with a satisfied nod.
When his men had all cleared out, he turned to look at
the remaining patrons scattered throughout the room.
There couldn't have been more than half a dozen remaining customers, most of whom were passed out at the tables near the back. The few that were still on their feet
made sure not to look directly at Bittermeyer unless the
owner looked at them first. As soon as he knew he'd
caught the man's eye, the customer would raise his glass
and look away again, hoping he hadn't drawn too much
attention to himself.

   Bittermeyer scanned the others with mild amusement.
He was happy to see that he could still command respect
from those who knew what kind of man he was. After all,
without respect, a man couldn't have much of a presence.
And without presence, that man couldn't impress himself
upon others. And once you could impress yourself upon
others, you could put the fear of God into them.

   That set of simple rules was how Bittermeyer lived his
life. He knew he wasn't the most popular man in town,
but he was the richest and the most feared. With that
knowledge firmly in mind, he lifted his glass to each of
the customers in turn and watched as they returned the
gesture while trying to hide the fear that seeped out of
them like the stink from a skunk's backside.

   The smell of fear was like rose water to Bittermeyer's
senses. It had the same, somewhat dirty, aroma of money
and the sharpness of sex. Every time he caught it in his
nostrils, Bittermeyer sucked it in and savored every last
whiff. He could smell it at that moment, which made his

newly refilled drink taste all the better when he tossed it to the back of his throat.

Bittermeyer's hand settled on top of the bar . . . *his* bar . . . and ran over the wood grain slowly, as though he was stroking the inside of a woman's leg. Already, he could picture what his men were doing to that loud-mouthed stranger who'd dared talking back to him in his own place.

The more he thought about it, the funnier it became. Finally, he was unable to contain himself any longer and a grim smile creased his lips.

Turning to Jones, he said, "Ever have one of those nights where every last little thing just goes your way?"

The barkeep was cleaning shot glasses with the towel that was normally hanging from his back pocket. "Sure," he replied with a nod. "Every man is blessed sometime."

Bittermeyer took another pull from his drink and let the whiskey crawl down his throat like a trickle of finely aged lava. Exhaling with a breath that should have been tinged with smoke, he said, "True enough, but not every man is quite as lucky as us. Take that stranger for example. My guess is that he won't be feeling too lucky at all in another minute or two." Already, Bittermeyer could hear that one's screams, as though he was right there when the first boots landed in the stranger's ribs. "No, sir. Not lucky at all."

TEN

For a moment, Clint was actually starting to forget about the verbal confrontation he'd just had with the owner of the saloon he'd visited. In fact, he'd even started to shrug off the constant flow of rain that never seemed to stop pouring onto his head and shoulders. All of that just seemed to fall to one side when he spoke to Belle. When her face lit up with a smile that had been forced down to the depths of her being, it was nearly enough to light up the entire street.

Clint followed her down the street and turned to see the redhead, Lucy, waving silently to them before turning to head back into the saloon. He and Belle were making their way beneath one awning and then another as though they were dodging the raindrops. They had made it to the end of the block and stopped to see which would be the driest path to take when a crashing sound came from behind.

At first, Clint thought it was another crack of thunder, but the noise was far too tame to be in the same family as the explosions that had been rocking the soggy night sky. He then thought the wind could have gotten ahold of a loose shutter, but his senses told him immediately that the wind was the single thing that had actually died down in the last couple of minutes.

All of these thoughts took less than a second to rush through Clint's mind, and when they'd run their course, they left an uncomfortable feeling in the pit of his stomach. "Just a second," he said to Belle. "Stay right here."

The blonde might have said something in response to his request, but the words were lost to Clint's ears as he turned around and peered into the shadows. The sound came again, but was more of a rattle this time. Now that he was waiting for it, Clint was certain that the sound could only be that of a door slamming shut, followed by boots slamming against the boardwalk.

Movement coming from the front of the saloon, combined with the sounds, gave Clint the entire picture. As he watched from his position beneath the awning of a storefront, he picked out the shapes of four men rushing in his direction.

It didn't take an eagle's eye to tell that they were the men that had been circled around Bittermeyer like a bunch of weasly parishioners. The only thing that bothered Clint was the fact that he could've sworn there were more of them inside the saloon, which meant that there were still one or two lurking about that he couldn't see.

"Clint, what is it?" Belle asked from where she stood behind him, with her back pressed up against the building.

Waving a quick hand in her direction, he said, "Stay right where you are. If you see the first sign of trouble, just get home as quickly as you can."

"But I don't want to leave you. You don't know Mr. Bittermeyer like I do. He could hurt you."

"Don't worry about me. Just do as I said." As he watched, the group of figures had already sighted him and were beginning to fan out and head directly for him. "Actually, why don't you just head on home right now. I'll catch up with you as soon as I can."

In the pouring rain and thick shadows, the figures seemed to drift in and out of sight like ghosts walking between headstones. As long as Clint focused hard enough, he was able to keep his eyes on them. All the while, he tried to catch any sign of the missing members of Bittermeyer's congregation. It was simply too much to hope for that all of the thugs would simply walk straight at him.

When he felt the hands on his shoulders, Clint's muscles twitched reflexively, his hand flashing to the Colt at his side.

"Be careful," Belle whispered into his ear while pressing up behind him. "Bittermeyer's men are killers, and he was right about there not being any law in these parts."

"Be careful on your way home," Clint whispered over his shoulder. "Keep yourself hidden as much as possible and wait for me. I'm going to have a hell of a lot of questions for you when I'm done here."

She kissed him on his neck and gave Clint hurried directions to her house before backing away and disappearing into the night.

Clint shook his head as the individual shapes became more distinct in the street ahead of him. He sure did have a lot of questions to ask Belle. And the more he thought about what he'd seen and heard since entering the town of Random, the more questions his mind churned out.

Just who the hell was this Bittermeyer person, anyway?

What power did he have over this town?

What exactly had he done to Belle and how many others had he treated the same way?

Shaking his head, Clint wondered why he kept sticking his nose into things that were none of his concern. Even before the question had gone all the way through his mind, he already knew the answer.

He did those things because they needed to be done. Men like Bittermeyer acquired whatever power they had because nobody else took the trouble to stop them. And even though Random was just a town in the middle of Oklahoma that had allowed one man to walk through it like some kind of power-hungry general, it was still full of people that deserved better.

At least, that's what Clint thought in the time it took for the group of men to come to a stop no more than ten feet in front of him.

The rain poured over their heads and ran down their faces, giving them all the appearance of stone statues that had come to life and gone out for a walk. They all had guns either on their hips or in their hands and stared across at Clint without trying in the slightest to hide the wickedness in their intentions.

Clint hoped that Belle hadn't stuck around to watch this the way she had back at the saloon. As much as he wanted to turn and check on her, he knew better than to take his eyes off of the four men for so much as a second.

A bolt of lightning tore through the sky, illuminating every man's eyes. Even though it was only for a moment, that one glance was all any of them needed to know that the air was about to be filled with a whole lot more than just thunder.

ELEVEN

"Not exactly the best night for a walk," Clint said as his eyes soaked up everything they could about the four men standing in front of him.

Each of the locals squared his shoulders and lowered his head to keep the rain from dripping into his eyes. One of them, a solid-looking black man on the end, spat on the ground before talking back.

"We ain't out for our health," the black man said. "And we sure as hell ain't lookin' out for yours, either."

All of the men seemed to get a bit of amusement out of that and allowed themselves to chuckle in response. Clint smiled, too, but not in a way that showed any humor. Instead, he used the momentary distraction to take a few steps toward the storefront. He knew that even the smallest advantage could mean the difference between life and death if the lead started to fly.

He'd managed to get a little closer to the wooden posts supporting the awning as well as the door that led into the building at his back.

"Yeah, that's a good idea," the black man said. "You'd best start backing away real fast. If you'd rather just turn tail and run . . . we wouldn't have any trouble with that either."

Another ripple of laughter worked its way through the men, but died off in half the time as the first. When they quieted down, the locals kept their eyes glued onto Clint, waiting to react to even the slightest move he decided to make.

Now that Clint was in as good a position as he figured he could get, it was his turn to square off with the others. The only difference was that when he did so, all the others froze like startled rabbits in a hunter's sights. There was no more laughter and there were no more boastful words coming from the quartet.

All that could be heard was the flow of water coming from the clouds and finding its way to the gutters, and the creak of wet timber shifting beneath Clint's feet.

"So did you boys come out in the rain for a reason?" Clint asked. "Or did you just feel like stretching your legs?"

This time, it was another man who replied. Standing next to the black man and wearing a long tan coat, this one clenched his jaw and gripped his sidearm a little tighter as he said, "We come to deliver a message."

"From Mr. Bittermeyer, I suppose?"

"That's right. He don't like bein' told off in his own place. And them that does such a thing need to be taught otherwise."

Clint's eyes narrowed as they shifted from one end of the row to another. Standing with his hips cocked slightly at an angle and his arms hanging loosely at his sides, he was still enough to blend in with the shadows and quiet enough to be mistaken for a distant rumble of thunder.

"And who's going to teach someone a lesson like that?" Clint snarled. "Just the four of you?"

His words hung in the air like a wasp floating dangerously close to the other men's eyes. Although they tried not to flinch, they couldn't keep their true fears from leaking out of them as though being squeezed from their very pores.

The rain seemed to get a little colder in the two seconds that drifted by.

The shadows grew just a little thicker.

"I asked you a question," Clint said in a voice that was heavy with the same bad intentions that the other men had been able to show up until a few moments ago. "Since it's you boys that are so strict on manners, you should either answer me or be on your way."

After years of playing poker, Clint could read another man's face easier than a Western Union telegram. He could tell that two of the men were about to toss their cards down and walk away. The man in the tan coat was still thinking about the hand he'd been dealt, but it was the black man who turned the tide of the game.

That one's eyes never strayed from Clint. They didn't blink and they didn't once look to anybody else for a cue as to what he should do next. There was no way to say for sure whether or not he was the leader of the group, but he most definitely was the first one that had enough sand to show his hand.

As it always happened whenever things went from bad to worse, Clint saw the world as though it had somehow slowed down and left him the only one who could move at a normal speed. The first thing he saw was the black man's hand clutching tight around his pistol and pulling it up from its holster.

When the others saw what was happening, they went for their guns as well, sending the entire situation straight to hell in a rush.

Even though the black man had been the first to start his draw, Clint was the first to finish. Without even having to think about what he was doing, his hand took hold of the Colt and brought it up in one smooth motion. As soon as the barrel had cleared leather, it was coughing out a plume of fiery smoke, sending a chunk of hot lead through the air.

By now, the black man was just starting to realize that he'd been outdrawn. As that terrible fact sank into his mind, Clint's bullet drilled into his chest, lifting him off his feet and sending him into the soupy mud that covered the ground.

The single gunshot rolled down the street, crackling between the buildings like a stray burst of thunder. As he fell, the black man tensed every muscle in his body, causing the gun in his hand to bark once before the life drained from his eyes.

As the body landed with a sickening thud, the window next to Clint was shattered by the dead man's only shot. When the next bolt of lightning struck, its light reflected off the broken window, where it was separated into a myriad of smaller bolts that radiated from the single hole near the door.

Instinctively, Clint dropped to one knee and focused on the three remaining figures. Part of his racing mind was hoping that they would be scared off. But those hopes were dashed as the next wave of gunshots went off, filling the air with lead that buzzed toward him like a swarm of angry hornets.

TWELVE

"That bastard shot Eddie!" the man in the tan coat hollered. "Shoot him down!"

Already, the remaining trio had snapped their hands up and taken their first couple of shots. The man in the tan coat and one other were holding pistols, while the remaining local had been cradling a shotgun in his arms like some kind of baby.

Even though they'd all started to fire, none of the men seemed to be levelheaded enough to think about where their bullets were going just yet. This was something that, even though he hated to count on it as a matter of course, had still saved Clint's life more times than he could count.

Any man could get lucky when his life depended on it, but good fortune rarely smiled on anyone stupid enough to live with a gun in his hands. Those kind of men needed to make their own luck, which was something that Clint Adams knew a hell of a lot about.

After dropping down to one knee to make himself a smaller target, Clint pressed his back against the door and inched a little closer to the shattered window. He could tell by the panicked moves they were making that the other men were far from professional gunfighters.

With that in mind, he also knew that they'd be pulling their triggers at anything they saw that remotely resembled a good target. Clint used this along with the storm to his advantage, moving himself close enough to the window so that the flickers of lightning threw his reflection onto the glass, where it was immediately broken into several other fractured images that might be just enough to throw a little more confusion into the mix.

All of this happened in the space of time between the first and second pulls of the locals' triggers. And since he had yet to feel the burning pain of a gunshot wound, Clint shifted his aim to the next figure in line, a clean-shaven young man between Tan Coat and the shotgunner who'd taken the initiative to step forward and get a cleaner shot.

The bullets were chewing up the air all around Clint's head and body as he tilted the modified Colt at just the right angle to pick off the approaching figure like a bottle from a fence post. Bucking once against his palm, the Colt spat its fire into the air and sent another soul into the great beyond.

His eyes opening wide and his mouth hanging open in silent disbelief, the young man looked down at the freshly drilled hole in his chest as his legs suddenly became too weak to carry his weight any longer. After letting out one final breath, every part of him relaxed and his body seemed to deflate like a falling pastry.

Clint knew that even the most panicked shooter would pull himself together eventually, and even though only a few seconds had passed, it was well past time to seek some real cover. His first impulse was to try the handle on the door behind him. Reaching with his left hand, he grabbed hold of the piece of metal and tried his luck.

Clint came up empty.

Something in the back of his mind screamed for him to get moving, and rather than look around for the cause of that feeling, he simply tucked his head in close to his chest and pitched himself off the boardwalk.

Clint felt as though he was falling through molasses. For the split second that he was plummeting toward the ground with his back turned toward the two remaining men, Clint swore that he was going to feel lead tearing through his flesh.

As the tips of his boots left the edge of the boards, he twisted his body and pushed off with the last bit of energy he could muster. The maneuver sent his torso into a tight spiral, which brought him faceup after what felt like an eternity, with his back turned to the firing line.

When he could finally see the gunmen once again, Clint lifted his pistol and squeezed the trigger two times in quick succession. He knew the first shot was going wide, and the only reason he fired it was to keep the two remaining men from descending on him the moment his back hit the ground.

That first shot had its desired effect and caused both men to take a few steps back even as they were about to empty their barrels out of sheer desperation. Tan Coat was just about to center his aim on Clint's body when he saw his target roll over in midair and fire back. That was more than enough to make the local man think twice about what he was about to do.

As for the shotgunner, that one had already blasted most of the glass from the front window's frame and was about to adjust his aim when he was forced to throw himself to one side at the sound of return fire.

Clint bent his right leg just enough to touch the ground with the bottom of his boot, which also cleared the path for the second round, which traveled the length of his body and clipped one of the locals in the shoulder, sending a stream of blood all down one side of the man's tan coat.

As soon as that bullet tore through its mark, the world shifted back into normal speed inside Clint's mind. It was just in time for him to bear the full brunt of his impact as his back slammed into a sloppy puddle at the mouth of an alley.

Suddenly Clint could feel the rain on his face and could hear the ringing in his ears as his senses snapped back to normal. His face was covered with muddy water that seeped into his mouth and nose, giving him the momentary sensation of drowning. He spat to one side while rolling closer to the bottom of the boardwalk, knowing full well that the shooters would be headed his way at any moment.

He sat with his back plastered to the wood and pulled the Colt in close to his body. Listening to the sounds of the approaching footsteps sloshing in the mud, Clint tightened his grip on his weapon. If he moved one moment too soon, he would give away his position and open himself up to return fire from both men. Even if he managed to take one of them down, the other would surely have plenty of time to take a free shot. And if he held off too long before firing, both men would get the opportunity to pull their triggers.

The local gunmen didn't have to be professionals to take advantage of poor timing. All they needed was to be capable of twitching their fingers upon the trigger out of sheer reflex. And since one of those men happened to be carrying a shotgun, the margin of error was cut down yet again on Clint's behalf.

THIRTEEN

Each of the men's steps echoed in Clint's ears. They were a little tentative, but still advancing toward his position. In his mind, Clint pictured where they would be standing and where their eyes would probably be focused.

The time for trying to move into a better spot was long gone. Now he simply had to make due with what he had. Even the slightest shift could have been a fatal mistake at this point. Even taking too deep of a breath could have been the one thing that caused those men to come around the corner just a little too fast or even start shooting through the planks of the boardwalk, where they might possibly get lucky by placing a bullet through Clint's skull before he could do much of anything by way of defense.

Even though he was going against nothing more than a group of local thugs who weren't even very good with their guns, Clint knew that his luck could turn right around and bite him like a poisonous snake if he wasn't careful. All he needed was for the men to take a few more steps and they would be right where he wanted them.

Just a few more steps and he would be ready to make his next move.

Right when he thought about that, Clint heard something that sent his heart racing and all of his plans to the brink of instant failure. It was at that moment that he heard the set of footsteps he'd all but forgotten about. Those steps didn't belong to the man in the tan coat or even the shotgunner.

They belonged to that fifth local that Clint had been looking for when he'd first spotted the group coming from the saloon.

And not only that, but those footsteps weren't coming from the same direction as the other men's. In fact, they were coming from the worst possible direction they could have chosen: from the end of the alley, which also meant they would be coming up behind Clint's position within a matter of seconds.

Just to confirm his suspicions, Clint glanced over his shoulder and was able to see the bulky figure of another man rushing toward him from the other end of the alley, catching Clint in a vice between himself and the remaining two gunmen from the original group of four.

Clint waited for another few seconds until one of the first shooters, the one with the shotgun, came barreling around the corner. The younger man gripped his weapon in both hands, his eyes wide and searching for something to shoot at.

The shotgunner might have been trying to speak, but all that came out of his mouth was a primal howl. The moment he laid eyes on Clint, he sighted down the sawed-off barrels and pulled down hard on his trigger.

Once again, Clint's instincts were sharp enough to take over the rest of his body in a frantic attempt to escape the wave of lead that was about to be unleashed in his direction. Rather that take refuge beneath the boardwalk, he rolled to the other side until his back slammed against the neighboring building. From there, he took quick aim and fired at the same time the shotgun filled the air with a deafening roar.

Lead whipped through the air to Clint's right like a deadly hailstorm. For a moment, he was certain he'd caught the brunt of the shotgun's fury, but he was somehow able to move and think clearly. When he blinked the smoke from his eyes, he could see the shotgunner reeling back and clutching his hand as blood flowed freely between his fingers.

Clint's hastily fired shot had bored a hole through the shotgunner's wrist. Although it was somewhat off of Clint's intended target, it was still enough to achieve the desired effect. The bullet had pulled the other man's aim at just the right moment, causing the shotgun's fire to blast a hole in the wall less than three inches over Clint's head.

When Clint scrambled to his feet, he could feel stinging pain lancing all down one side, biting at him like a row of fire ants. He ignored the sensation and quickly looked around him, hoping that the gunfire had blasted some sense into the remaining shooters.

Unfortunately, although the local gunmen were obviously shaken by the fiery exchange, none of them were ready to give up just yet.

"Nobody else has to die," Clint said in a last-ditch effort to avoid any more bloodshed. "Walk away now and this can be over."

The newest arrival stopped while still inside the alley. He looked to be the youngest of the lot, but was easily the biggest. Clint recognized the man as one that must have been seated next to Bittermeyer in the saloon. The guy was so tall, however, that he had appeared to be standing at the time. Now that he was on his feet, he seemed to fill up the alley like a giant crouching in the mouth of a cave.

FOURTEEN

Before Clint took his eyes away from the bigger man, he saw the local step from the shadows and raise a gun in one hand. It was at that moment that Clint realized a good part of the giant's bulk wasn't his own. In fact, the massive figure had been clutching something close to his chest that hadn't been visible until he stepped a little closer.

Huddling against the local thug and enveloped in one of his massive arms, Belle shivered uncontrollably when the hand wrapped around her throat thrust her out and held her in place as though she was on some kind of display.

"Look at what I found," the big gunman said. He started to smile, but that expression quickly gave way to a snarl when Belle tried to wriggle free from his grasp. "Stay put 'or you're the first one to die."

Clint straightened his back and fixed the big man with a steely gaze while making sure to watch the other two from the corner of his eye. "She won't be the first," he said in a menacing tone. "Take a look around you."

The giant started to chuckle, but then caught sight of the bodies lying on the ground. He also saw that his two remaining friends were wounded, their blood mixing in with the rain as it coursed down to the mud at their feet.

Clint could see that his words had taken their toll upon the giant. Even though the local was bigger than Clint and had a hostage for more leverage in a tight spot, he was obviously new to a real fight and was shaken up by the sight of his friends' blood.

"You harm one hair on that woman's head," Clint warned, "and I'll make sure that I burn you down before you know what hit you."

Desperation mixing with outright fear, the big man's eyes widened into white-rimmed saucers and the gun in his hand twitched between Clint and Belle. "Y-you're outnumbered, mister. Eddie . . . are you all right?"

Clint glanced over to see what the others were doing. While the shotgunner struggled to pull a holdout pistol from his boot with his wounded hand, the man in the tan coat was using trembling fingers in an attempt to reload his pistol.

"Eddie's dead," Clint said. "If you play this right, you don't have to follow him."

It seemed as though it took a few moments for the notion of his friend's death to sink into the big man's skull. He glanced at the bodies again and tried to get the others' attention. Finally, he saw that the two lying on the ground were never getting up and something cracked inside of him.

Clint knew his time to talk his way out of this was quickly running out. It wouldn't be too much longer before one of the remaining men screwed up the courage to take another shot at him. And once one of them started firing, the rest would follow suit.

At that moment, Clint heard the definitive *snap* of Tan Coat's cylinder being flicked into place.

"Last chance," Clint said.

His answer came right away in the form of another pair of sounds as both Tan Coat and the giant thumbed back their hammers and got ready to fire.

Clint looked first to see if he could tell where the giant was aiming. As soon as his eyes turned toward the big man, he was looking down the local's barrel. Since that meant that Belle wasn't in immediate danger, that was just fine with him.

Next, Clint launched himself into action, twisting his body in a blur of motion to take down the shooter who seemed to be more collected than the rest and, therefore, a bigger threat.

The Colt bucked in Clint's hand, sending a round into Tan Coat's face just as the gunman was about to squeeze off his shot. The older man's head snapped back as his finger reflexively clamped on the trigger. His gun went off in his hand, but his arm had already dropped so that the bullet dug a hole into the wet ground near his feet.

In a flash, Clint had turned to face the giant, who still had his hand around Belle's throat. The big man was screaming something, but his words were lost amid the raging gunfire.

"Belle," Clint shouted. "Down!"

Covering her head with both hands, the blonde dropped straight down and dangled from her captor's hand as though she was swinging from the branch of an old oak tree. She shut her eyes tightly and lowered her head as much as she could in an attempt to hide herself from the hell that had broken out all around her.

Clint wasn't sure if she had heard what he'd said or if Belle was merely reacting to the sound of his voice. All that mattered was that she did manage to give him a clear shot. Already, the giant was bringing his gun up and sighting down the barrel with wild, murderous eyes.

Just to be absolutely sure, Clint gave the big man one more second to put down his weapon. Once that had ticked away, Clint pointed his finger and pulled the Colt's trigger. His final bullet left its chamber in an explosive blast.

Before the sound could fully register on the giant's senses, his mind had already been sent to oblivion. The big man's entire body convulsed once, his grip tightening dangerously around Belle's throat.

For a moment, Belle thought that the life was about to get squeezed out of her. She tried to take in a panicked breath at the sound of the gunshots, but was unable to get any air past her captor's grip. Just when her vision started to blur, she felt the grip loosen and then the hand fell away completely.

Before she knew what was even going on, she felt the tears start streaming down her face.

"It's all right, Belle," Clint said as he reached out to pull her away from the giant's falling body. "Everything's going to be all right."

The moment she opened her eyes and found herself in Clint's arms, the blonde buried her face in his chest. Instead of springing from fear, her tears were now those of relief.

FIFTEEN

The shotgunner watched with panicked eyes as the rest of his group was cut down in front of him. In all the times he'd been sent out to kick down the door of a small business who hadn't paid Bittermeyer his due or beat the tar out of some stubborn landowner, the local gunman had never once thought that his life could possibly be in danger.

In all that time, it had been he who'd held all the cards and the rest of the town that was afraid of what he might do to them. He'd gotten to recognize and even savor the smell of fear that drifted from the bodies of those who begged and pleaded for mercy.

Now, one more time, the smell of fear drifted into his nostrils. But it wasn't coming from some stammering old man or some kid who'd been battered to within an inch of his life.

This time, he was the one who gave off the stink. It was his sweat that took on the pungent aroma that he'd gotten to know so well. And they were his muscles that trembled uncontrollably as he fumbled about to try and do something to protect himself against the inevitable.

Clint watched the wounded shotgunner's attempts to pull his pants leg up over his boot. Even a task as simple as that seemed to elude the trembling man, however, and he simply couldn't seem to get to the small holster that was strapped to the top of his boot.

"Are you going to be all right?" Clint asked for what must have been the third or fourth time.

Belle took a deep breath and finally managed to stanch the flow of tears. After wiping away the salty moisture from her eyes, she nodded meekly and stepped away from Clint. "I'll be fine. Just give me a minute to collect myself."

Nodding, Clint leaned in and kissed her gently on the cheek. He was reassured by the determination that was evident in the woman's eyes and posture. Even after what she'd just been through, Belle seemed to be handling herself rather well.

Clint turned his attention back to the last remaining gunman, who was just now starting to tug at the leather strap that kept what looked to be a small .32 in place on his leg. There were only three steps separating him from the shotgunner, and Clint covered those in the space of a heartbeat. On his fourth step, he lifted his boot and brought it down hard on the gunman's wrist just as the other man had managed to free his pistol.

Even with his hand pinned to the ground, the shotgunner still tried to cock the .32's hammer back. He almost made it, until the boot on his wrist pushed down even harder and every one of his fingers suddenly went numb.

Clint stood looking down at the gunman. When the other man reached for his shotgun with his free hand, Clint swept his other boot in a sharp kick that sent the weapon spinning into the shadows.

The gunman tried to pull his hand free, but couldn't move it even a fraction of an inch. He then looked up at

Clint, eyeing the Colt, which hung from his hand like the grim reaper's scythe.

"I know what you're thinking," Clint said. "You're wondering if I need to reload or if I just might have another round left in the cylinder. Well, if you help me out just a little bit, then you won't have to concern yourself with such details."

"A-and if I don't?" the shotgunner asked, using up his last bit of defiance.

A morbid smile drifted onto Clint's face, followed by a subtle wink. "If you don't, then we'll have to answer that question the hard way."

The shotgunner looked down at the Colt one more time as the images of his friends getting blown off their feet flashed through his mind. He attempted to think about how many times that Colt had gone off, but was unable to come up with a number that was a sure enough bet to risk his life upon.

In the end, the gunman let out the breath he'd been holding and plopped into a sitting position on the ground. When Clint lifted his foot slightly, the shotgunner nearly fell backward. His hand had already turned a dark shade of purple.

"I just work for Bittermeyer," the shotgunner spat out. "Odd jobs and such. I can't do anything for you."

Clint didn't holster his pistol, nor did he so much as point it toward the man at his feet. Letting it hang right where it was seemed to be doing a great job of flustering the other man, so that's where he kept it. "Why were you sent after me? Was it just for what happened back at the saloon?"

"Yeah, yeah. Mr. Bittermeyer said you needed to be taught some respect."

Nodding, Clint said, "That's simple enough. And I suppose Bittermeyer owns a good piece of this town and runs it how he sees fit."

"That's right."

"And how do you think he'll react when he gets wind of what happened here tonight?"

The fear in the shotgunner's face doubled in half a second. The smell of it pouring off of him started to mingle with a different kind of stench that made the entrance to the alley smell more like an outhouse.

"I'm not the first person to be on the receiving end of a reception committee like this one, am I?" Clint asked.

Reluctantly, the shotgunner shook his head.

"How many people has Bittermeyer killed?"

"I—I don't know."

Clint only moved his head a fraction of an inch, raising his eyebrows in a nonverbal warning.

The shotgunner picked up on the facial cue immediately and raised his hands as though another boot was coming for his face. "It's the truth, mister! I know Bittermeyer's done plenty to certain people, but nobody knows how much. Some say he was a hired gun years before he even came to Random."

Just then, Clint felt a hand on his elbow. The touch was gentle and unmistakably feminine.

"I can tell you plenty about Bittermeyer," Belle said from behind Clint. "Let's just please get out of here before anything else happens."

Clint nodded and bent down to pick up the .32, which still lay in front of the shotgunner. With a flick of his wrist, he opened the small gun's cylinder and dumped the cartridges into the mud. He then tossed the pistol under the boardwalk and turned to walk away.

"One more thing," Clint said as he slowly turned back around to face the man lying in the mud. "I want you to deliver a message to your boss. You think you can do that for me?"

The shotgunner nodded again as though his head was on a spring.

"I want you to tell him that he should treat visitors a little better. If he wants to keep running this little kingdom of his, he should be a little more careful to make sure he doesn't upset the wrong people or draw too much attention to himself. Be sure to tell him that he's done both with this little display here tonight. And now that he has, his problems have only just started."

And with that, Clint turned his back on the other man and continued his walk toward the other end of the alley.

"Hey," the shotgunner called out before Clint could get too far.

Clint glanced over his shoulder and waited quietly.

"You can't leave me like this. Once Bittermeyer finds out I failed, he'll know I told you the things I did. And once he knows all that . . . I can't rightly say what he'll do to me."

"So, after all you and your friends tried to do to me tonight, I should give a damn about you being in trouble with your boss?" Clint asked incredulously.

The shotgunner slowly climbed to his feet and held his hands where Clint could see them. "That's not what meant. I need to know . . ."

Suddenly Clint understood what was being asked of him. "Oh, you want to know about this?" he said while holding up the Colt.

Shrinking back slightly, the shotgunner nodded.

In one fluid motion, Clint turned on the balls of his feet and leveled the pistol so that he was aiming directly at the other man's head. After waiting for half a second, he slowly squeezed the trigger.

Sweat poured off the shotgunner's face in a stronger flow than the rain as the Colt's hammer leaned back . . . and then . . . snapped forward toward the back of the cylinder.

Click.

Clint smiled as all color drained from the shotgunner's face. The local's consciousness followed soon after, causing him to faint dead away.

"Let's get going," Clint said to Belle, who'd been watching the entire thing through wide eyes. "I think I'm done here for now."

SIXTEEN

Alonzo Bittermeyer stood in the front doorway of his saloon, leaning against the frame as though he was just calmly watching the setting sun. Except there was no setting sun and there wasn't a part inside of him that was even close to being calm.

He'd listened to the crackle of distant gunfire while sipping his drink. Since the fight was too far down the street for him to see it, he could only imagine what his men were doing to that smart-mouthed stranger who'd decided to give lip to the wrong man at the wrong time.

Whoever that man was, he deserved what he was getting. At least, that's what he thought when he'd been listening to the shots from afar.

Once the sounds weren't enough to appease his curiosity, Bittermeyer had taken a stroll through the rain to get a look as his men finished that stranger off.

That's when he'd seen it.

Eddie's body was lying on the ground. That much wasn't too big of a surprise since the kid really hadn't been able to prove himself in real combat until now. It wasn't until he saw Maher take a shot to the head that the

61

full realization of what was happening hit Bittermeyer like a fist wrapped in cold steel.

Maher had been the veteran of the group and a real force to be reckoned with among Bittermeyer's personal army. Now the experienced gunman was dead in the mud, his tan coat soaking up rainwater and blood alike. That sight flashed in Bittermeyer's eyes, illuminated by the jagged crack of lightning that tore through the sky amid a clap of thunder.

Bittermeyer jogged a few steps closer just so he could get a look for himself at how something like this could possibly happen. His question was answered right away when he saw the stranger moving like a shadow from a damn nightmare and twice as fast as the lightning in the sky. The big one, Kade, had managed to get ahold of the blonde whore, but even that advantage didn't do him any good.

Once he saw the stranger dispatch all of them but Stanton, Bittermeyer turned his back on the alley and walked toward the comfort of his saloon. He stood at the bar and waited for the inevitable gunshot, but it never came. Instead, all he got was the patter over his head of rain that seemed to have been falling for more than an eternity.

By the time he finished the drink that had been set in front of him, Bittermeyer heard a set of footsteps clomping on the boardwalk and headed toward the saloon's front door.

Although he hadn't seen too much of the stranger, Bittermeyer knew that the footsteps were too hurried to belong to that one. No . . . those steps were quick and rushed. More than that, they were scared. Bittermeyer didn't have to hear much to sense that fear.

He could smell it.

SEVENTEEN

"Mr. Bittermeyer," Stanton hollered as he burst through the door. "They're dead, sir. All the rest of them are dead."

"And I guess you just barely managed to escape with your life. Is that right?"

"Well . . . yes."

"And what did you do with that shotgun you're always carrying around?" the saloon owner asked. "Did you manage to fire it or did you just throw it at the stranger before you pissed a yellow streak down your leg?"

Stanton stood in the doorway, his hands on the frame, as though that was the only thing keeping him upright. "I fired at him . . . we all did . . . but it wasn't enough. That stranger was too fast."

Draining his drink, Bittermeyer felt the whiskey filter down his throat to settle among the rest of the alcohol he'd consumed that night. Although the liquor was making his muscles warm and loose, the intoxication wasn't half of what he wanted it to be. Years of indulgence had strengthened his tolerance to almost legendary degrees.

Now, rather than gain any enjoyment from his drinking, Bittermeyer only found himself getting number and meaner with every sip he took. "Is that so?" he asked while turning to face the other man.

Recognizing this turn of mood, Jones walked to the opposite end of the bar and motioned for his younger apprentice to do the same. Both barkeeps tended to the few remaining customers and assured them that their next round of drinks was on the house.

Bittermeyer didn't care about anyone in the place beside the man in his sight. Stalking forward with his hands on his hips, he glared at Stanton and stepped up so that there was no more than three feet between himself and the other man.

"You say the stranger was fast?" Bittermeyer said.

"That's right, sir. He was—"

"Shut up!"

Stanton bit his tongue and tried to step all the way into the saloon. His progress was stopped by a look from Bittermeyer that was so stern it might as well have been a brick wall dropped in front of his path.

Bittermeyer closed the distance with a pair of slow, deliberate steps. Not once did he take his eyes away from Stanton. And when he planted his feet, his gaze bored all the way through to the back of Stanton's skull.

"I don't give a shit how fast that stranger was," Bittermeyer seethed. "I sent you to do a job and I expected you to do it. You should know me well enough to know what I expect of the men I employ." After a tense moment of silence drifted by, Bittermeyer took a deep breath and continued. "Now, did he get the message I sent along with you all?"

Stanton's head bobbed up and down like a cellar door in the middle of a windstorm. "Yes. Yessir, he sure did."

"Good. Now that's a start," Bittermeyer said with a beaming smile. "And as your reward, you may come into this saloon and have a drink to warm your bones."

For a moment, Stanton looked as though he didn't quite know what to expect. He stood in the doorway as the rain soaked his backside, eyeing his boss like a forlorn puppy. When Bittermeyer finally took a step to one side and motioned for him to enter, Stanton walked into the saloon and peeled the jacket from his soaking shoulders.

Snapping his fingers, Bittermeyer said, "Jones, get this man a drink. Can't you see he's drenched?"

The senior barkeep fixed a glass of whiskey and set it on the end of the bar. After that, he turned and made his way back to the opposite side of the room.

Bittermeyer waited for Stanton to take a few healthy sips before clapping his hand on the other man's back. "All right. You managed to do the first thing I asked you to do, now do you happen to remember the rest of your job?"

Stanton gritted his teeth as the whiskey chased away some of the chills that had settled into his bones like a wet fog that had been piped directly into his body. "Yessir, I remember."

"And what was that?"

"We was supposed to teach him some respect."

"Did you?"

Taking another drink, Stanton put his foot up on the rail beneath the bar and leaned his elbows onto the smooth wooden surface. "We told him he was out of line when—"

The impact of Bittermeyer's fist on the bar was enough to make Stanton jump just as high as the glasses resting in front of him. "Did you teach him some respect . . . yes or no?"

Those last words echoed through the saloon and brought everything and everybody inside to a complete standstill. For a moment, even the rain seemed to hold off in deference to Bittermeyer's rage.

Stanton stepped away from the bar and stood in front of the saloon's owner with his hat in hand and head down low. Judging by the way he presented himself, he seemed to be one second away from dropping to his knees before the other man.

When he spoke, it took every bit of Stanton's strength to keep his voice from trembling. Even so, his words hung precariously in the air like a soap bubble getting ready to pop on the end of a child's finger. "I think that he knows better than to—"

"That's not what I asked you!"

"Sir, that stranger should know better after what—"

Stanton's sentence was cut short by a stiff backhand that smacked into his jaw and snapped his entire head to one side. When he looked back at Bittermeyer, his first impulse was to strike the saloon owner back, but once he saw the look in the other man's eyes, he quickly stashed that reflex deep in the back of his mind.

Glaring angrily into Stanton's eyes, Bittermeyer was tensed and ready for anything that might happen. His fists were balled up tightly in case he had to strike the other man again, and his arm was ready to go for the gun in his shoulder holster.

In a way, Bittermeyer might have been somewhat impressed if Stanton did put up even a little fight. But as it was, he could see the other man's courage fading away just as quickly as it had come. And in the next second, Stanton had lowered his head like a frightened puppy.

"Now," Bittermeyer said, "think carefully this time. Did you, or did you not, teach that stranger any respect?"

Wiping at a trickle of blood that had come from his lower lip, Stanton wasn't sure if the wound was new or simply one that had been reopened from his scuffle in the alley. He knew for sure that the loose tooth he felt was definitely new. "No, sir," he said meekly. "I don't believe we taught him any respect."

"There now," Bittermeyer said in the closest he could get to a soothing voice. "That wasn't so hard, was it?"

When Bittermeyer took a step toward the man, Stanton reflexively flinched away. But this time, the saloon owner brought up his hand a little slower so he could take hold of Stanton's chin. "That's not so bad," he said while examining the man's battered face. "I'd say you got off pretty light compared to the rest of your group."

"Y-yessir."

EIGHTEEN

Even though Belle's house was almost on the other side of town, the walk there didn't seem like much of a chore at all. After spending the better part of the day being spit on by the never-ending storm that seemed to be permanently hanging over his head, Clint actually found the trek through Random to be somewhat relaxing.

The rain had let up a little bit and was now just a heavy spray on Clint's face, which served to wash away some of the tension that had been drilling through his body after being jumped and shot at in the alley. The cool wind blowing over his soaked clothes was more effective in waking him up than any amount of coffee he could have had. But before too long, his muscles started to shiver and the chills wrapped their clammy arms around him like a possessive ghost.

"Here it is," Belle said as they approached a small cottage at the end of a row of similar structures.

The houses looked as though they'd been spaced much farther apart at one time. But since Random had grown, the spaces between the first homes were filled with newer ones to accommodate the town's fresh arrivals. All of the buildings were simple in design and were sectioned off-by split-rail fences. Most of them were dark at this time of night, but they all still seemed somehow inviting.

Belle lifted the latch to her door and stepped inside, motioning for Clint to follow. As soon as they were both out of the rain, Belle shut the door and walked over to a small pot-bellied stove, where she immediately began preparing a fire.

Once the warmth started flowing from the blackened steel, Belle darted about the room to light a couple of the lanterns that were scattered here and there. By the time the place was fairly well lit, the stove had banished most of the chill back out where it belonged.

Clint looked around and saw that most of the cabin was taken up by this one room. Besides the stove, there was a large table with three chairs, a pair of cupboards and a rack of pots and pans hanging from one wall. A couple barrels of dry goods were in one corner and on the opposite side of the room was a small rocker next to a sewing basket.

There was also a narrow doorway, which probably led to a bedroom. The air inside the cottage smelled of fresh bread and wet cedar. All in all, it was one of the most comfortable places that Clint had been in for quite some time.

Peeling off his jacket and draping it over a hook next to the front door, Clint sat down in one of the chairs next to the table and scooted in closer to the stove. "So, Miss . . ."

"Yates," she said quickly. "My full name is Isabelle Yates, but all my friends call my Belle."

"Does that include Mr. Bittermeyer?"

Averting her eyes while setting a teapot on top of the stove, she shook her head. "No. Not anymore."

"I'm sorry, Belle. I didn't mean to pry. It's just that I tend to get a little curious about somebody when they send a group of hired guns to try and kill me as soon as

I pull into town." Extending his hand, he added, "My name's Clint Adams."

She took his hand and shook it gently. "Not at all, Clint. If anyone should apologize, it's me. I'm the one that got you into this whole thing to begin with."

Clint watched as she stood next to the stove with her arms folded tightly across her chest. She was a beautiful woman, but there was something looming around her, a darkness, that clouded her picturesque features and made her draw within herself.

"I'm making some hot tea," she said. "I hope that's all right."

"That's fine."

"I've got some biscuits and honey. There's also a slab of beef out back that I can cook for you if you'd prefer."

"You know what I'd prefer?" Clint asked. "I'd really prefer it if you sat down and took a rest for a little while. You look more beat than me, and I've been riding all day and dodging bullets all night."

When Belle looked at Clint, she saw that he was smiling at her and pulling out the chair next to his. After pulling down a pair of tin cups and some tea from one of the cupboards, she finally dropped herself into the chair and let out an exhausted breath.

"There," Clint said. "Now, isn't that better?"

Belle nodded.

"If you don't want to talk about Bittermeyer right now, you don't have to. In fact, if you don't want to talk about anything, that's fine with me. You have a fine home and I appreciate just being in out of this rain for a little while."

After a few seconds of silence between them, Belle fixed her eyes on Clint and cleared her throat. "Actually, I'd like to talk about what happened tonight," she said. "I'm fairly new in town, myself, and I really don't have anyone else to talk to."

Clint had seen enough hurt in his life to recognize when someone was filled with it. Although Belle was doing her best to put on a strong front and get on with her life, there was a fresh wound just beneath her surface that was causing her a great deal of pain. He could see it in the way she was afraid to lift her chin or speak too loudly. Most of all, he could see it in the way she held herself with her arms tightly wrapped around her. It was almost as though she was protecting herself from an attack that was still going on in her mind.

"I can tell you're not like most other men," she said, her eyes examining Clint just as he was examining her. "I've barely spoken to you, but I feel like I can already trust you. After all, nobody else would have lifted a finger to help a . . . someone like me . . . the way you did. Not in this town, that's for damn sure."

"Why not?"

"Because of Mr. Bittermeyer. They know that if they do anything he doesn't much like, they'll be dead before they get a chance to regret it. And as much as I appreciate what you did for me," Belle said with a tremor in her voice. "I'm afraid that you're in for the same thing. Maybe worse."

NINETEEN

"Now . . . last question." Bittermeyer waited until he knew that Stanton's eyes were focused solely on him before continuing. "Did you find out anything about this man?"

By the way his eyes shifted back and forth and his mouth opened and closed, it was obvious that Stanton had something to say, but just wasn't sure if he should actually say it. Finally, he nodded and pulled away from Bittermeyer's grasp. "He wasn't just some smart-mouth cowboy. He was fast with the iron and moved . . . like nothing I've ever seen before."

"Is that so?" Bittermeyer turned to lean against the bar. "Go on."

"He's got to be some kind of gunfighter. He went through all of us like we was barely even there. Even Maher."

Nodding, Bittermeyer thought back to what he'd seen near that alley. Something seemed vaguely familiar about this stranger, but he still couldn't quite put his finger on what it was. The more he heard about him, the clearer the picture in his head became.

He felt like he was right back there, watching his men drop like scarecrows cut from their posts.

"He . . . he let me go, sir."

That seemed to snap Bittermeyer out of his thoughts. "What was that?"

"The stranger. He let me go."

"Why?" Bittermeyer asked without the slightest bit of compassion or tact.

"He told me to deliver a message . . . to you."

Cocking his head to one side, Bittermeyer raised his eyebrows with genuine amusement. "He did, now? Well, what was this message that was so damn important?"

For a moment, Stanton began to panic as he searched his memory and came up with nothing but a blank. But when he thought back to when he'd been sitting in that cold mud with the storm raging overhead, and staring down the barrel of that Colt, every last detail crystallized in his mind.

"He said that you should be more careful if you wanted to run this place all by yourself." Pausing, Stanton waited for another backhand across his mouth. When it didn't come, he took a deep breath and forged ahead. "Also, he said that a man like you shouldn't piss off the wrong people or draw attention to yourself."

Bittermeyer stared straight ahead. Although his eyes were sharp and focused, he didn't see the man in front of him or even the inside of his saloon anymore. Instead, his thoughts went back to the alley down the block. Stanton's words floated around him like voices from the past.

"Is that all?" Bittermeyer asked.

"He said you made a big mistake tonight. And if you ask me, sir, I'd have to say he was right."

When Bittermeyer turned to look at Stanton, his eyes were filled with so much rage that it seeped out of him like wisps of steam. Instinctively, his hand went for his gun, but froze the moment his fingers touched its handle.

In the next few moments, every eye in the saloon was on Bittermeyer, waiting to see what he was going to do.

Even though the general consensus was that Stanton was a dead man, not a single person in the place was about to lift a finger in his defense. Instead, they all just watched like they were about to see one hell of a show.

"What did you just say?" Bittermeyer asked.

It was at that particular moment that Stanton realized he'd just made a very big mistake. "N-no disrespect or anything, b-but all I meant was that Maher had been telling you that same thing for a long time."

"That's true, isn't it. And, tell me, when did you become such a fucking keen observer of detail? Or did I just manage to knock something loose with that last swat I gave you a moment ago?"

After taking a look around at all the people who were staring at them, Stanton leaned in close to Bittermeyer and braced himself for the potential outcome of what he was about to say. "Me and Maher were talking the other day about . . . all that's been going on in town over the last couple of weeks or so. He made me swear not to say anything, but—"

"Maher's dead," Bittermeyer hissed. "And unless you want to be hot on his heels, I'd suggest you get to the point."

"It's that deputy, sir. Maher . . . and some of the rest of us . . . think that it might not have been a good idea to treat him the way you did."

Nodding, Bittermeyer said, "Ahhh. I see. So the lot of you got together and grew a brain. Is that what you've been doing with all the free time in your lives? Well, let me put that brain at ease and tell you that what happened to that deputy was necessary. You know why?"

Before Stanton could have a chance to answer, Bittermeyer said, "Because I said so. And in this town, that's the only thing that carries any water whatsoever. If you live or die, it's because I say so. If a store stays open or burns to the ground depends on my say-so. And nothing anybody else says makes a damn bit of difference within the limits of Random. Am I understood?"

Stanton nodded.

"Good," Bittermeyer said through clenched teeth. "Now I want those bodies taken out of that alley so my fellow townspeople don't have to see their faces when they step out for breakfast, and I want you to do it. When you're done with that, go find the others and tell them its time to earn their money. I don't give a rat's ass how fast that stranger is, he needs to see that the day he drove his horse into my town was the worst day of his entire life."

Stanton couldn't believe it. Somehow, some way, he'd managed to sidestep a death sentence. His features relaxed as though he'd been thawed out, and he let out a lungful of air. "Sure, Mr. Bittermeyer. I'll bring them all right here as soon as I can."

"Not till tomorrow morning. Let them get their sleep. They're going to need it."

TWENTY

"When I first met Alonzo Bittermeyer, I thought he was the nicest man I'd ever seen in my life," Belle said after she'd fixed cups of hot tea for herself and Clint. "He was handsome, charming, intelligent and worldly. I was working in San Francisco at the time, at a house run by a woman who was more of a sister to me than any kind of boss."

Clint sipped at his tea, which felt like a warm blessing running through his cold body. "So you were a . . ."

"Patsy used to call her girls entertainers, but the rest of the world called us whores," she said without the slightest bit of shame in her voice. Now that she'd had a chance to relax inside her own home, Belle seemed to be letting more of her true self shine through. "We made an honest living no matter what some of the holier-than-thou types would say. It was a damn sight better than being a politician, I can tell you that much."

Caught off guard by the woman's sudden turn of mood, Clint nearly spat out some of his tea when he started laughing at her easy humor.

Allowing herself to laugh a little as well, Belle placed both of her hands around the warm cup and glanced at

Clint from the corner of her eye. "Have you ever been to San Francisco?"

"Yes. Several times. It's a beautiful city."

"It sure is. And if you've been there, then you've probably been to Patsy's place. It was called the Bay Club."

Clint shook his head. "Afraid not. I don't normally find myself in need of those kind of services. At least . . . not so I'd have to pay for them, anyway."

Belle's rich blue eyes took in Clint as though she was soaking him up one piece at a time. "No," she purred. "I guess you wouldn't."

For a couple of seconds, the two savored the moment that was passing between them. That, combined with the hot tea, served to warm them both up enough that they didn't seem to feel the effects of their rain-soaked clothes any longer. It was Belle who broke eye contact, however. And when she did, she did so reluctantly; her eyes drifting down over Clint's chest and then back to her own hands.

"I had a good life in California," she said before too long. "I was saving up for a club of my own. Patsy was even going to help me get started."

"That's very . . . enterprising," Clint said. "What made you change such a good plan?"

"I didn't change it. I just . . . put it off for a while after being talked into leaving San Francisco by a man named Alonzo Bittermeyer."

Rolling his eyes, Clint said, "Yeah, I got to witness that one's charm firsthand."

"He told me that he ran the biggest places in Random and that this town was on the verge of becoming something truly big. A 'Mecca of the South' is what he called it."

"I've heard talk like that before. Actually, it was from a man named P. T. Barnum. He had a nasty habit of talking things up too. As I recall, he used that to make quite a good living for himself."

Belle nodded. "I've met Barnum as well. And if a sucker's born every minute, then you're looking at one right here," she said while hooking her thumb back at herself. "After several nights of expensive dinners and fine wines, Bittermeyer talked me into coming all the way across the country so I could work at his biggest saloon.

"The deal was that I'd get a chance to open up my own place after profits got high enough in his. You see, I've got a nose for business and I managed to double Patsy's income in a matter of one year."

"Impressive," Clint said with a nod. What he found more impressive than that was the way Belle seemed to come alive more and more with each passing second. The more she talked about her dreams and aspirations, the more she seemed to snap out of the sullen trance that had darkened Belle's features since Clint had first seen her.

"I thought so," she said while running her fingertips along the edge of her cup. "Maybe that's what made me so blind to what was really going on. It kind of reminds me of another famous saying: If something looks to good to be true . . ."

"Then it probably is," Clint finished.

"Right," Belle said softly while letting her gaze drift away from Clint. "It most definitely is. I found that out the day I arrived in Random. The Rosewood is a beautiful place, there's no denying that. And when I saw it the first time, I thought that working there would almost be too good to be true."

Clint was about to ask her about the Rosewood, but then he realized he'd never gotten a look at the name painted onto the front of Bittermeyer's saloon. He assumed it was the Rosewood since that was the first place he'd seen both Bittermeyer and Isabelle Yates.

Still looking down at her hands, Belle continued her story as the energy that had been in her words only moments ago was already draining out of her. "I was to work as his assistant. At least that's what he told me on the train ride from California. And I even got started in that direction until he started . . . changing.

"When he looked at me, I could tell he wanted something more than sound business advice. To tell you the truth, I was thinking along the same lines." Her eyes flicked up to meet Clint's for just a moment, a look of subtle shame crossing her face. "It wasn't love. Just . . . attraction between two people who'd been spending a lot of time together."

"That's nothing to be ashamed of," Clint said as he reached out for Belle's hand.

"Maybe not. But I've lived my life by my own rules for some time. Doing what I do for a living may not be the most prestigious thing in the world, but it allowed me to sock away a lot of money over the years. Most women my age need to find themselves a rich man to do that well for themselves. And all those years I was making money and doing what I had to do, I thought for sure that I knew how to look out for myself and protect my interests." The energy was coming back into Belle's voice, only this time it was more of an aggressive kind of energy that flushed her cheeks and lit a fire in her eyes.

"As soon as I started working for Alonzo," she said. "I realized that I wasn't going to be used for any of the projects we'd talked about back in San Francisco. I was just going to be . . . used. He'd seen what he wanted and did everything he could to get his hands on it."

"The money you saved?" Clint asked.

Belle nodded. "That's right. He took every last penny and told me it would be used to build up the town's newest gambling parlor. That was the one he would turn over to me eventually once the whole thing got set up properly. The truth of the matter was that he never intended for me to be anything but another whore in his stable. Maybe not one that would be hired out like the rest, but his own private diversion that he would use whenever he was in the mood for a laugh."

"When did you realize all of this?" Clint asked.

"About a week ago." Laughing, Belle shook her head and looked up at Clint with intensely burning eyes. "I overheard him talking to his men. Apparently, he didn't trust me anymore after what happened to that deputy that passed through here not too long ago."

Clint's ears perked up at that last part, since it seemed to be so out of place with the rest of what she'd been saying. "Deputy? What deputy?"

TWENTY-ONE

Belle examined him for a moment or two, studying him as though she couldn't decide if he was serious or not. "The deputy from Oklahoma City. The one that was sent here to act as the town law until Random voted its own sheriff into office."

"So what happened to him?"

"You really don't know?" she asked in disbelief.

Shaking his head, Clint locked his eyes on her and said, "No. I don't know. Why don't you tell me."

After what he'd seen of Bittermeyer so far, Clint had a sneaking suspicion that whatever Belle was about to say, it wasn't going to be good.

Taking a deep breath, Belle furrowed her brow and got up from her chair. She walked to the stove and picked up the teapot which was still simmering over a hot burner. "From what I heard, Random was a small town that didn't attract much attention until recently. Once it boomed, the place started drawing more visitors as well as the attention of some government type who passed through on his way north. Well, he decided that Random was getting too big to go without law and he sent a deputy to keep an eye on things. You ask me," Belle said while lowering her voice

as though there was actually someone else there to over-
hear what they were saying, "I think the deputy was sent
to keep an eye on Bittermeyer more than anything else."

"Really? Why?"

"Bittermeyer's had his scrapes with the law. Even got
his hands into a couple train robberies that turned awful
bloody. Nothing the railroads could prove, but even in
San Francisco there seemed to be folks keeping tabs on
him."

Clint nodded and let all this information sink in. "If he
did get away with railroad money, he'd be the target of
some of the best investigators money could buy. And just
to cover all their bases, the railroad would also put a price
on his head to entice as many bounty hunters as possible."

"I may not be too knowledgeable about this subject,
but if there was evidence against him, wouldn't the law
just arrest Bittermeyer?" Belle asked.

"If there was evidence, sure. But the railroads might
have gotten their hands on some information that wasn't
enough for a court to go on. A private business could do
whatever they want with it. Bounty hunters aren't exactly
deputized representatives."

"True enough."

"And all the railroads would care about is either getting
their money back or putting away the man who took it.
Did you say there were people after Bittermeyer in San
Francisco?"

Belle shook her head while sipping her tea. "Not exactly. It was more like they were watching him."

"Who was watching him?"

"I don't know for sure. Some shady types. I didn't really think anything of it since, in my kind of business, I
come across all types of men. Some of my best clients
were shady types. They were the best tippers, anyway."

Every couple of minutes, the picture in Clint's mind
regarding Random, Oklahoma, was changing, like a pic-

ture cast on the surface of a rippling pond. The more he heard about Bittermeyer, the more he understood what was probably going on inside the man's head. More than just some self-important bully, the owner of the Rosewood saloon was turning out to be a genuine threat to the people living in this town.

It was obvious that he had a group of followers who jumped whenever he snapped his fingers. And it was also plain to see that Bittermeyer was awful quick to snap those fingers. Also, for a man to feel that secure when wanted by the forces at the command of the railroad barons, he would have to have a fairly large amount of his own resources as well.

"Can I ask you something, Clint?" Belle said.

The sound of her voice snapped Clint out of his own thoughts and brought him back to the present. "Go right ahead," he replied.

"What are you here for? In town, I mean. Why did you come to Random?"

The moment Clint thought about his response, he couldn't help but laugh. "Just like the name says. It was luck. Nothing but dumb luck and one hell of a storm."

Hearing that, Belle managed to laugh a bit as well. "Then I guess the town's name is pretty fitting. After all, if my luck had been a little different, I would never had met Alonzo in the first place. He would have seen another girl's face in Patsy's place and he would never had gotten his hooks into me."

TWENTY-TWO

Even though Lucy had seen the entire scene play out in front of her eyes, she still couldn't quite believe it. Standing in front of a darkened storefront, huddled in the same shadow that had concealed her from everyone that had passed by the alley across the street, she tried once again to dredge up the strength to move. And once again . . . she failed.

It was getting so late that she thought the sun might be starting to make itself known at any moment. And even after a full day's work, she couldn't allow herself to drop down on the ground just to take a load off her aching feet.

She was still too scared to rest.

Too scared to breathe.

The only thing that got her to move was the sound of footsteps coming down the street, sloshing through the puddles, and heading for the alley she'd been staring at for what felt like an eternity.

Even when she closed her eyes and turned her head, she could still see the bodies lying amid the river of blood flowing around them. The gunshots still echoed in her mind no matter how hard she tried to block it all out.

Finally, when she caught sight of Stanton making his way toward the bloody mess in front of the alley, Lucy found the strength to move away from the door. For a moment, she was worried that Stanton would find her, but it was soon obvious that the gunman wasn't even trying to look for anyone and was more concerned with the bodies themselves.

Once she saw Stanton bend down next to one of the corpses and start dragging it to one side, Lucy knew it was safe to make a break for her freedom. Each step that she took thumped like an anvil being dropped onto loose boards, but only in her own mind. She thought that Stanton would surely hear her as she tried to get away and even made the mistake of stopping once or twice to check if she'd been spotted.

Only one time did Stanton almost spot her, and that was only because she'd been taking so much time to creep away. The gunman turned away from his task for just a second, his eyes glancing toward the other side of the street at the same time Lucy had paused to see what he was doing.

If he'd been searching for bystanders, Stanton would surely have found her. But he was only trying to clear his lungs of the stench of death before squatting down and pulling another corpse out of the alley. The gunman muttered silently to himself, grunting the occasional curse under his breath while going about his task.

The moment she saw Stanton look away, Lucy jumped from the boardwalk and landed on the balls of her feet in the alley opposite from the one where Stanton was working. As soon as her feet hit the ground, she tiptoed down the alley and emerged at the rear of the row of buildings. Once there, she was certain she'd put enough distance between herself and the gunman, so she took off at a full run, simply to get away from the gruesome scene.

After a few seconds, she stopped and thought about what had happened.

Before the terror could sweep over her again, she put the bloody images out of her mind and thought, instead, about what she should do next. After all that had happened, she didn't think she'd be missed at the Rosewood. At least, not until her next shift.

And since she'd been diverted from what had dragged her out into the rain in the first place, Lucy decided to check on the one person who seemed to be just as deep in this as she was: Belle Yates.

With a destination firmly in mind, Lucy quickly got her bearings and cut across to another alley closer to the end of the block. As she moved, she could hear more people coming down the street, followed by the sound of men's voices shouting back and forth to one another as they converged near the scene of the gunfight.

Although she was too intent on running to focus on what the men were saying, Lucy recognized the voices as belonging to some more of Bittermeyer's men. Unlike the ones that hung out at the Rosewood as much as the local drunks, these men were the ones that weren't seen until things really started getting bad.

Lucy had heard those voices a couple times while working at the saloon, and every time, they sent a chill down her spine. The men they belonged to were like the specters of death. Whenever they showed their faces around Mr. Bittermeyer, blood was soon to flow.

She knew she had to see if Belle had somehow managed to get away. And after that, Lucy knew she had to find someone who might actually be able to stand up to Bittermeyer and his killers. There had to be someone who could stop the flow of blood that had started running straight through the town of Random.

After what she'd seen in the last hour or so, Lucy knew just the man for that job.

TWENTY-THREE

Something was still gnawing at the back of Clint's mind. And now that Belle seemed to be calmed down and willing to talk about things, he figured that it was as good a time as any to clear the air. "Now I've got another question for you. If I'm out of line in asking it, just let me know and I'll understand."

Once again, the shadow crept over Belle's face and she lowered her head just enough to keep herself from meeting Clint's eyes. "Go on."

Clint felt bad for bringing the darkness back to her lovely face, but still needed to ask his question if he was to put his mind at rest. "What happened earlier tonight between you and Bittermeyer? It looked to me as though you two were—"

"Actually," she cut in, "we had just finished what you thought we were doing."

Rather than push Belle for more information right away, Clint let her take her own time. It seemed like she was ready to talk to him, but just needed a moment or two to collect her thoughts. After a few deep breaths and another sip of tea, she looked up and nodded.

"Bittermeyer and I were lovers. We had been ever since the first time he saw me in San Francisco. Of course, it started out as more of a business transaction, but wound up being something more. At least, he thought it was something more."

Clint detected a trace of guilt mixed in with Belle's words. It was something more than regret or even pain. It made her shake her head like someone who'd been caught red-handed doing something they'd been warned several times not to do.

"Patsy told me to keep the customers at a distance," Belle said. "Some men get love confused with lust and . . . Alonzo was one of those men. I could tell that the minute he started talking to me, and that was part of what brought me all the way out here at his side."

Suddenly, the rest of the picture snapped into focus for Clint. "So you were planning on using him while he was using you?"

"That's right. It seemed like an average business relationship, but when I saw Alonzo's more . . . shady side, I thought that would make it all the easier for me to get close to his fortune and start taking bits of it for myself."

"And last night?"

"Last night . . . well, let's just say that Alonzo proved he wasn't quite as blinded by my beauty as I thought he was. We got together like every other night and he started asking me questions about what I really wanted from him and what I was up to. When I didn't answer right away, he started getting . . . violent. And when I tried to calm him down, it seemed like he knew exactly what I was thinking and what I'd been trying to do." Belle paused for a second while wringing her hands and then smoothing the front of her skirt. "He said that I was his property and that I had to be put in my place. He told me that I was only good for one thing."

Clint could feel his temper coming to a boil inside his chest, rising up through his body like lava inside a volcano. Biting back his growing rage, he asked, "Did he rape you?"

To his surprise, Belle answered the question with a smile. "That's the funny part. He didn't rape me. He didn't even try to hurt me . . . not right away."

Clint's rage simmered down and was immediately replaced by confusion. "Then what did happen?"

"He . . . had his way with me and I had my way with him. It wasn't until we were finished that I realized what was really about to happen." She turned her back to him now and spoke over her shoulder. Reflexively, her hand drifted toward the cut on her neck, which now looked just like a scrape beneath her chin. "I thought I'd really put one over on him. I thought I'd beaten him and that I could steal what I could and then run away in a day or two. But after he . . . marked me . . . he put his clothes on, looked at me . . . smiled . . . and winked." Turning around to face Clint again, she added, "I'd seen that smile before. It was the same smile he gave to that deputy . . . right before he ordered his men to slit his throat and bury the carcass outside of town."

"Do you think Bittermeyer will do the same thing to you?" Clint asked.

"If you would've asked me that question back in San Francisco, I would have told you no. I thought I could outsmart him or get away before anything too bad could happen. But after the things I've seen . . . after what Bittermeyer has done . . . I'd say he's just waiting for a good time to plant me next to that deputy."

Belle's voice trailed off, but Clint didn't mind. He'd already gotten more than enough to paint a picture in his mind. Although he'd been guilty of making a snap decision about Bittermeyer, Clint felt like he had more pieces to get a better look at the whole.

"So where are the rest of them?" he asked.

"The rest of who?"

"Bittermeyer's men. If he's capable of half of what you say he is, that means he's got to have better help than what he threw at me tonight. I need to know how many of them there are and where they hide out."

Belle paced the room for a few seconds, moving like an animal that had only just realized it was inside a cage. Before too long, she came to a stop and looked at Clint. "Since there isn't much hope for me by this point, I guess there's no harm in telling you everything there is. After all, Alonzo can only kill me once, right? There's a bunch that hangs around him. But there's also some others. Two of them that were different. I only saw them once or twice," she said. "Actually, only one time for sure. The other time, I wasn't certain if it was one of them or not."

"Were they hired guns?"

Belle thought about that for a second and then shook her head. "I don't think so. They seemed too . . . professional for that. I've seen my share of hired killers . . . Patsy used to keep company with some pretty rowdy types . . . but they had a certain air about them.

"These men that were with Alonzo seemed to be . . . colder. Almost like they killed folks just because they liked it. Not just because they were getting paid for it. And Alonzo treated those two more like partners than workers."

To anyone else, the distinction might have seemed unusual or even too small to make a difference. But Clint had seen that type of man plenty of times, himself. And when a man picked up a gun to use it as a tool to feed himself and family or even bring in outlaws for the price on their heads, it was a world of difference from that same man picking up a gun out of sheer pleasure.

That was the difference between bounty killers and murderers.

A pure-blooded murderer was a frightening sight to behold. They didn't have any sign of humanity in their eyes unless they were inflicting pain on someone else. They killed because they'd acquired a taste for it. And they would never stop.

Not until they were put in the ground.

"Yeah," Clint said softly. "I know the type."

"When the one I saw was in town, he stayed at one of Bittermeyer's smaller places. A cathouse called Gracie's on the east end of town. The other man stayed there too. I didn't see him doing anything, but he had that same stink about him as the first man. And when he left town, the bodies of some of Alonzo's enemies turned up . . . in pieces."

TWENTY-FOUR

Suddenly Clint was overcome by an uneasy feeling. It wasn't something based on what he'd just been told. Instead, it was more of a general uncertainty he had concerning Belle Yates. He could see that she was obviously going through no small amount of pain, but it was also plain to see that she wasn't the type who was used to being completely up front with anybody.

Those things, he knew from way too much past experience, could add up to a very dangerous combination. Once they'd finished their tea, Belle excused herself to her room. Although she'd let him know he was more than welcome to sleep in her place, Belle left it up to Clint if he was going to pick a chair or crawl into bed next to her.

She didn't seem opposed to either one, but just to be on the safe side, Clint took a third option and left her little house completely.

When he stepped outside, Clint was happy to see that the rain had finally let up. It would be several more hours until the sun rose, but already it felt like a brand-new day. Simply being able to lift his head and look up into the sky without getting a mouthful of water was enough for

Clint to feel like celebrating. Instead, he decided to find himself a room where he could feel safe and get some much needed sleep.

He folded his jacket over his arm and started walking back to the main part of town. Before he could spot any hotels or rooms for rent, Clint saw a figure running from building to building, stopping at every door and ducking into the shadows.

Whoever it was, they were making their way toward him, so Clint decided to cut through the mystery and meet this new arrival head-on.

"No need to hide," he said in a stern voice. "You're not very good at it, anyway. Just come on over here and tell me what you're after."

For a moment, the figure stayed put. Pulling back further into the shadows, it kept perfectly still as though hoping that Clint would forget it was there. But after a few moments, it stepped away from the building and then rushed toward Clint at full speed.

Clint's reflexive response was to go for his Colt. But the instant he caught sight of the figure's face, he stopped himself before clearing leather.

Lucy's striking red hair had been the one thing that saved her hide more than anything else. It was this that Clint saw first. Otherwise, he might have tried to defend himself before the waitress even got close. Once he held back, Clint allowed her to run up to him, wrap her arms around his midsection and squeeze him as tightly as her arms would allow.

"That's a good way to get yourself hurt," Clint said once her initial excitement had subsided.

Lucy pulled away, but didn't let go. Looking up at him, she started to shake and then moved to look beyond him. "I came to see Belle," she said. "Did she get away all right?"

"Yes, she's sleeping in her own bed. What happened to you?"

After a few deep breaths, Lucy relaxed and took a seat on the edge of the boardwalk. Once she started to speak, the words spilled out of her like a rushing waterfall. "I wanted to make sure she got home safely, but one of Bittermeyer's thugs followed us out of the Rosewood. He cut us off before we made it too far and shoved me down and then grabbed hold of Belle and dragged her away. I tried to do something or even fetch some help, but he already had a knife to her throat." Suddenly, her eyes brightened and she tensed up again. "It was Kade! That's the man's name. It was Kade and he said he was going to—"

Clint moved his hands to her shoulders and then stroked the back of her neck. "It's all right," he said. "I know what happened next. I was there."

Leaning her head against Clint's palm, Lucy let out a relieved sigh. "Thank God. And what about Kade? He said there were going to be plenty of others to take . . ." She stopped for a second and looked at Clint intently. "He said they were going to take care of you."

"They tried. They just didn't do a very good job, that's all. Where did you go after Belle was taken?"

"I tried to go back to the Rosewood, since I thought you might be there. I wanted to warn you, but Bittermeyer had so many men around and they were all carrying guns. I was . . . afraid. After I heard the shooting, I went to see what happened and saw all the bodies lying there . . . bleeding."

Just then, she grabbed onto Clint once again and buried her face against his shirt. Lucy pressed her body close to his and moved her hands over his chest. "I thought they'd killed you. I thought they'd shot you and left you in the mud. Before I could see for sure, some of Bittermeyer's men came to take away the bodies. That's when I decided to come back here. I would've made it sooner, but I wanted to be sure nobody saw me."

Standing so close to her, Clint got a good, long look at Lucy's face. Her skin appeared to be luminescent in the dim light of approaching dawn. Wide green eyes stared back at him as the pink tip of her tongue darted out to moisten her full, rose-petal lips.

The energy coming from Lucy was much different than Belle's. Clint could feel her muscles tensing against his body, writhing as though every part of her yearned to touch every part of him. She was a slender little thing, but she was full of life that seemed to radiate from her like the sun's auburn rays.

"You did the smart thing," Clint said. "From what I hear, Bittermeyer may not be out for good, but he's certainly done for the night."

"Nobody's ever stood up to him like that. Well . . . not so they could talk about it afterward." She held his gaze and let her body melt against Clint's. The attraction that had only been hinted at back at the saloon was now coming to full bloom. There was no denying that both of them could feel the energy that seemed to crackle between them.

"I need somewhere to stay for the night," Clint said. "Someplace safer than one of the rooms at the Rosewood."

Lucy bit her lower lip and pretended to think long and hard about Clint's predicament. Finally, she nodded and took him by the hand. "I've got just the place in mind. It's close by, has a nice warm bed and comes with a hot meal when you wake up."

"What about the service?" Clint asked with a smirk.

"Well, there's only one waitress there, but I know she's going to take extra good care of you."

TWENTY-FIVE

Lucy's house was just a bit smaller than Belle's, but had a much warmer feel to it. Situated in an area that had an equal number of tents and shacks among the more well-constructed dwellings, the little cabin was just a single room cut down the middle by a curtain hanging from the ceiling.

There was a fireplace in one corner near all the cooking supplies, as well as a small table that looked as though it might have been pieced together from scrap lumber. Although it was somewhat rough around the edges, it had been touched up enough by its owner to feel like a true home. The only problem was that it was a little too close to the Rosewood for Clint's liking.

"What do you think?" Lucy asked as she led Clint inside and took his jacket.

"It might have been a better idea to go somewhere a little farther away from the viper's den, if you know what I mean."

Dismissing his concern with a wave of her hand, Lucy removed the shawl that she'd been wearing and draped it over the back of a chair. "Mr. Bittermeyer provides homes for his employees. I got this one because I've been working for him for so long. In all my time serving drinks in that saloon of his, I don't think he's stepped foot in this part of town once. Some of my neighbors think he doesn't know or even care where his workers live, just so long as they show up for work in the morning."

Just being out of the rain had caused Clint's clothes to dry somewhat. His shirt wasn't sticking to his skin quite so much, but it was still a layer of cold and damp around him. "That seems like a . . . nice thing to do."

Lucy shrugged. "It's just his way of keeping us dependent on him. Everybody knows that, but you know what they say about biting the hand that feeds you. Here," she said while stepping up close and tugging at the top buttons of Clint's shirt. "Let me get these things off of you."

Her hands drifted like a gentle breeze over his body, plucking the buttons open one at a time until she could remove the shirt from him completely. As she worked, Lucy's body brushed against him, her own clothes still cold and moist as well.

When he looked down at her, Clint could see the nipples growing hard at the ends of her pert little breasts. Lucy's thin white shirt clung to her flesh, exposing every curve of her stomach. The line of her neck was highlighted by the trails of red hair that stuck to her in thick strands.

When she stepped back, Lucy soaked in the sight of Clint standing in front of her. She kept his shirt in her hands and then let it drop to the floor. Reluctantly, she turned away for just a moment. "You're soaked to the bone."

Clint stood in place, enjoying the way Lucy moved within the clinging confines of her own clothing. Her dark cotton skirt held onto her smooth, slender hips. When she turned just the right way, the light from one of the room's lanterns fell over her backside to highlight each sloping curve.

She seemed to feel that she was being watched, and when Lucy walked over to a small cedar chest, she bent deeply at the waist and shifted her hips in just the right way to make the breath catch in Clint's throat. Opening the chest, she fished out a folded towel and walked back to where Clint waited.

"Here," she said, while pressing the towel and her hands to Clint's body. "How about we get you dried off a little before climbing into bed." As she moved the towel up and down over his muscles, Lucy smiled warmly and looked up into his eyes. "How's that?"

Clint allowed himself to be tended by the redhead, lifting his arms or turning slightly whenever prompted. "That's very nice," he said. The strain of trying to hold himself back was coming through in his voice.

When she heard this, Lucy smiled even wider and moved around to dry Clint's back. Her arms massaged his shoulders through the towel before slipping around his waist. "Funny . . . you don't seem so cold anymore."

Clint reached around to slide a hand over Lucy's hip. She squirmed slightly in response to his touch, her breasts pressing against his back.

"I don't feel so cold anymore," Clint said. "If fact, it's getting awful warm in here."

Lucy draped the towel over Clint's shoulders and stepped around so that they were facing each other. Her fingertips slid down his ribs and went immediately for his belt buckle. "Well if you're hot, then maybe we should get you out of these," she said while unfastening his pants.

While she worked slowly at his jeans, Clint removed Lucy's shirt. The wet cotton held onto her like it was reluctant to let her go. Beneath the filmy material, she wore nothing but a thin layer of water that had seeped in between the garment's weave. When her shirt joined

Clint's on the floor, Lucy closed her eyes and let out a contented sigh.

"Mmmm," she purred. "Now I feel like I'm getting hot."

Clint's hands were already slipping beneath the waistband of her skirt, easing it down over her hips until it was just about to drop to the floor at her feet. He could feel his jeans coming loose and Lucy's hand sliding beneath the denim to stroke his hardening penis.

When he felt her hand close around him, Clint all but tore Lucy's skirt from her body. He stopped trying to hold himself back one moment longer and allowed himself to indulge as his instincts dictated.

First, one hand went around to cup her tight, rounded backside, while the other moved to the warm patch of hair between her legs. Then, after pulling her in close, he started rubbing the sensitive nub of her clit before slipping one finger over the lips of her vagina.

Lucy moaned softly, her hips grinding back and forth to guide Clint's touch. A soft, rumbling moan eased up from the back of her throat.

"I may not have been in Random for very long," Clint said, "but I can tell you one thing for sure."

Lucy's lips brushed along the nape of his neck, working their way up to close around his earlobe. "What's that?" she whispered.

"You people sure know how to make a man feel welcome."

TWENTY-SIX

The sky was beginning to brighten, giving the illusion that daybreak was drawing near. But the sun had a few more hours left before it was set to arrive, and for the most part, the town of Random was still dead asleep. Some parts of it, however, were just plain dead.

Stanton craned his neck and tried to work out some of the kinks that had settled into his back. Overhead, the black storm clouds that had been hanging over everything for most of the week were actually drifting apart to reveal the stars and moon that had been hidden like a treasure stashed away in the heavens.

It was these things that made the sky seem unusually bright. The moon was only three-quarters full, but its light was so much brighter in comparison to the underbelly of the thunderstorm, which was finally packing up and heading out.

"This ain't what I get paid for," came a scratchy, rasping voice to Stanton's left.

The man who'd just spoken stood an inch or so shorter than Stanton. His sinewy body was covered with layers of tattered clothes and a ragged duster. Glaring with narrow, intense eyes, he picked up a shovel that he'd been working with and tossed it to the ground at Stanton's feet. After cracking his knuckles loudly, he reached up and scratched a cheek that was covered with several week's worth of dark stubble.

"You get paid to do what Mr. Bittermeyer says," Stanton retorted. "So just help me do it and we'll be on our way."

The men were standing on the outer edge of Random's graveyard. Most of the markers in the main part of the burial ground were finely carved or even chiseled from stone. In the section where the two men stood, on the other hand, the markers were nothing more than planks shoved into the earth. Occasionally, someone had bothered to fashion one of them into the shape of a cross, but those were more the exceptions than the norm.

Nodding slowly, the scruffy man took a step toward Stanton and locked eyes until the other man looked away. "That's right," he rasped. "I take orders from Bittermeyer. Not you." One gnarled hand drifted toward a scabbard that hung from his belt and went all the way down to his knee. All he had to do was draw the machete out an inch or two before he saw Stanton hold his hands out in front of him.

"Jesus, Connor, what the hell do you think you're doing?" Stanton sputtered.

"I'm showing you the difference between them that digs graves and them that fills 'em," Connor said in a drawling hiss. The blade glinted in his hand with the solemn promise of slow death. It felt cold pressed up against Stanton's throat. And when he dragged it against the other man's skin, Connor savored the whimper that gurgled in the back of Stanton's throat.

"All right," Stanton said once he was able to compose himself somewhat. "I'll finish up the digging."

"That's right, you will. And the next time the boss man tells you to drag me outta my bed, you'd best nod like a good little doggie and then forget you ever got the order. Understand?"

Stanton tried to nod, but the motion brought his jugular uncomfortably close to the machete's edge. So instead he drew in a breath and said, "Yeah. I understand."

"Good," Connor grunted as he withdrew the machete and turned to leave. "I guess I'm through here, then."

Before he could get too far, he was stopped by Stanton's raised voice.

"Wait!"

Connor froze and then turned around as though he was about to lunge for the other man at any second.

"There's more we got to do," Stanton said. When he saw the look in Connor's eyes, he quickly added, "Not just this bullshit. Real work. Your kind of work."

"Oh? And just what kind of work is that?"

"The man who did this," Stanton said while motioning toward the pine boxes lying on top of or beneath the mud. "Mr. Bittermeyer wants him found and punished for what he done. He said you and Paul should search every inch of this town until you find him."

"And then what?"

"Well . . . I guess that's up to you."

Connor stood still for a few seconds as his mind raced with all the twisted possibilities he could dredge up. As he thought, his thumb traced lightly over the handle of his machete and he licked his lips like a hungry dog. "This fella's still here? After all that happened, he's still somewhere in Random?"

Stanton nodded. "Mr. Bittermeyer thinks so, and nobody's seen him leave. I checked the stable myself and his horse is still there."

The smile on Connor's face didn't hold so much as a drop of joy. Instead, it was a demented caricature of a grin that would have looked obscene if worn by anyone else. On him, it looked positively frightening. "That one's gotta have some set of balls on him if he does this and don't even got the sense to leave town. He can't be just some cowboy who rode in for a drink and a roof over his head."

"I don't know who the hell he is, but Mr. Bittermeyer wants him hurt. And before you do anything too bad—"

"I know, I know. We won't kill him until the boss man is there to watch. We done this enough times to know how it goes."

With that, Connor turned and started walking out of the shoddy cemetery. Stanton watched him go as his feet sunk a little deeper into the freshly turned mud. The ground made a wet, sucking sound as he pulled his feet from the grime, and another deeper sound when he was forced to plant them right back in.

Two fresh graves were to his left, each one marked by nothing more than a pile of mud and half a broken board. Two more caskets were waiting to be buried, and now Stanton would have to do the grisly job all by himself. His eyelids were heavy with fatigue, but he forced them open with thoughts of how it would feel to pass out and find himself facedown in this burial ground.

His most sobering thought, however, was of what was going to happen to that stranger once Connor and Paul got their hands on him. Sure, the stranger had killed four of Stanton's friends, but no man deserved the hardships that those two killers put men through. Just thinking about it made the chill in Stanton's body feel like a warm tropical breeze.

TWENTY-SEVEN

The door to Gracie's came flying open amid a thunderous crash and a hail of splinters. The cause of the crash was easy enough to find, since the fat man's body didn't seem naturally suited to flying through the air, no matter how much he flapped his arms and squawked.

Landing in a heap with his arms and legs akimbo, the fat man kept right on squawking, his words slurred from too much alcohol as well as a swollen, bloody lip.

"And don't ever show yer ugly face around here again!" shouted a tall, muscular man who filled up the shattered door's frame.

The man still on his feet stood a few inches over six feet and had smooth, olive-colored skin. He wore dark trousers held up by black suspenders and a plain white shirt with sleeves rolled up just past the elbows. His thick, dark hair was pulled into a tail at the back of his head and held in place by a leather strap.

Behind him, one of Gracie's working girls poked her head out, soon to be followed by another onlooker who was curious to see what was about to happen to the fat man. Soon, the entire doorway was filled by women in various states of undress.

"Kick his ass," one of the girls said. "That fat man thinks he can slap me around, but he's got another thing coming!"

Nodding, the tall man with the ponytail rubbed his hands together and cracked his knuckles before stepping outside. "Is that a fact, now? You think you can lay a hand on one of these fine ladies."

Rolling onto his belly, the fat man propped himself up and spat out a mouthful of blood. "I paid for that whore. I can do whatever I want to her."

Towering over the portly figure, the tall man cocked his head to one side. "Afraid not," he said before sending the toe of his boot into the fat man's ribs. "You'll just have to save the rough stuff for somebody else."

He gave another kick to the same place, only this time it seemed to sink in just a little deeper.

"Then again," he continued. "After I'm done, you might just become a pacifist." A stomp straight down onto the fat man's head. "Or a toothless lump of lard without the ability to walk."

The beating continued for another solid minute. Although that stretch of time might not have seemed like much on any other occasion, this just happened to be the longest sixty seconds of the fat man's life.

And he was unconscious for twenty of them.

When he was done, the tall figure was drenched in sweat and his boots were slick with mud and gore. He knelt down and delivered one last downward jab to the other man's face for good measure. And when he stood back up, rubbing his knuckles and breathing heavily, he found the doorway full of stunned, quiet faces.

"What's the matter?" he said to the working girls. "You all act like you never seen me work before."

One by one, the women's faces disappeared. Leaving the fat man to rot in the mud, the tall figure stepped onto the boardwalk and through the front door.

The inside of Gracie's was standard fare for a brothel: thick carpeting and walls covered with dark paper and mirrors; a small bar on one side of the front parlor, next to a velvet sofa. Most of the women had gone back to their rooms. All except one, who sat on a customer's lap, brushing her fingers along his gristly chin.

Walking up to the bar, the tall figure glanced once at the customer and nodded. "Hello, Connor. Back for another round already?"

Connor's hand rested on the girl's thigh, rubbing slowly up and down. "Maybe in a bit. But first we got some business to take care of. That is, if you didn't waste all your energy on that pig outside. You look tired, Paul. I thought I'd never see the day someone like that would take so much out of you."

Paul downed his drink in one swig and flexed his bloodied hand. "You want to see how much I got left, then you're welcome to try me, little man."

Sending the girl on his lap away with a sharp swat to the behind, Connor let out a rasping laugh and got to his feet. "Save the talk for the ladies. This job's being handed down from the boss man, himself. Remember those shots we heard earlier tonight?"

"Yeah."

"They were coming from the Rosewood, all right, but five of Bittermeyer's local buddies got shot up. Only one is still walking and he's burying the other four. The one who did it is still in town."

"Hah," Paul grunted before licking off some of the blood from his knuckle. "This should be fun. Any idea where he is?"

"Not yet, but I know somebody who should. I got a girl who works for Bittermeyer that owes me a favor. She's at that saloon of his every night of the week and sees every last thing that goes on there. If something like this happened, she knows about it. And she also knows to find out as much as possible for when I come calling."

Paul nodded, leaned over the bar and fixed a drink for Connor as well as a refresher for himself. "You sure you can trust this bitch of yours?"

"Sure," Connor said while accepting the drink. "Why wouldn't I? What're you so skittish about?"

"No reason. Just that, whoever this is, he took out five men and walked away without a scratch. Just seems like we should know a bit more about him before we go barging through his door."

"I saw the bodies. They weren't full of holes. Just clean shots. Heart or head. Even Maher got put belowground."

Paul took a little more time with this drink. He sipped the liquor while nodding to himself. "Then we've got a real gunfighter on our hands. Maybe someone faster than the old man, himself."

Smiling, Connor said, "That's exactly what I was thinking. Since we don't know exactly who we're up against, I think we should give him a test. Maybe throw some of the local boys against him so we can see what happens for ourselves."

"And once we size him up, we cut him in two."

TWENTY-EIGHT

Lucy walked backward, leading Clint by the hands to her bed on the other side of the room. All the while, she kept her eyes locked on his, her lips parted in a seductive, expectant smile. Lowering herself down onto the mattress, she pulled Clint down on top of her and slid one leg up around his hips.

Watching the slender redhead move was a pleasure for Clint. Her body slithered through the shadows like a feather drifting through the air. Her hands grew hot and insistent as they freely explored every inch of his body. He felt himself growing harder by the second as she slid one hand between his legs and stroked him gently.

"I want you to touch me," she said softly. Lucy took Clint's hand and guided it to her pussy. "Right there. Mmmm, that feels so good."

He looked down at her face, savoring the way she closed her eyes, leaned her head back and enjoyed his touch on her most sensitive areas. After a few more seconds, he did some exploring of his own, slipping his fingers inside of her and then rubbing them along the lips between her legs.

Lucy's eyes clenched shut even tighter and she pressed the back of her head into her pillow. Moans of passion began filling her throat and soon she was squirming beneath him in sheer pleasure.

Sliding his fingers in and out of her, Clint could feel drops of moisture dripping between Lucy's thighs. The moment he slid out of her, Clint lay down on the bed and looked across into Lucy's eyes. Without saying a word, he lifted his wet fingers to his mouth and took a quick taste as she watched.

The moment she saw this, Lucy smiled widely and rubbed against Clint's hard body. "You like that?" she asked.

"Oh, yes," Clint replied. "I wish I could taste some more of it right about now."

Before the words could get all the way out of Clint's mouth, Lucy was on her knees and straddling Clint's chest. Once there, she reached down and rubbed the sweet spot between her legs and then brushed her fingertip over his chest.

Clint couldn't wait any longer. Reaching up with both hands, he grabbed hold of her hips and pulled her toward his face. Lucy took a moment to turn around so she was facing his legs before scooting back and lowering her pussy down onto his waiting mouth.

Lucy grabbed hold of Clint's ankles and tossed her hair back the moment she felt his tongue slip inside of her. Every muscle in her body strained as she cried out with waves of ecstasy. When she was able to open her eyes again, she looked down at his stiff cock and lowered her head so she could devour it.

Her full, pink lips closed in around his column of flesh and her tongue swirled around its head. Sucking gently, she took him all the way into her and held him there before moving her head up again. She bobbed up and down in the same rhythm Clint was using as he ran his tongue between her legs.

Reaching up to hold Lucy's tight little ass with both hands, Clint tasted her pussy and nibbled lightly on the inside of her thighs. He could feel her mouth working over his penis, and every time she swallowed him down, fiery sensations coursed throughout his entire body. He used the intense feelings to speed his own efforts and buried his tongue deep inside of her.

Gripping the base of his shaft in one hand, Lucy threw her head back and let out a shuddering cry when she felt Clint's tongue penetrate her tight vagina. "Oh God," she moaned. And then her climax pulsed through her flesh in tumultuous waves that caused her to buck on top of him until they finally passed through her.

When she was at last able to move again, Lucy crawled off of Clint's face and moved down his body. Settling over his rigid member, she lowered herself down until she could feel the head of his cock pushing in between her legs. A few gentle shifts of her hips and he was inside of her. Lucy groaned loudly as she lowered all the way down, taking every inch of him deep inside of her body.

From his position, Clint could see Lucy's back as she began riding his cock in a steady up-and-down motion. Once he started pumping up into her as well, she leaned back and stroked his chest with her fingernails. Clint reached up to slide his hands around to her breasts, squeezing her erect nipples between thumb and forefinger, which caused her to cry out even louder.

Lucy's slender body dropped back onto Clint's chest, her hips grinding back and forth as he drove in and out. She then reached behind her to stroke Clint's face. Every time he fully penetrated her, she screamed with intense pleasure, her entire body quaking with a second and third orgasm.

Just listening to her cries was enough to drive Clint to the breaking point. Reaching around her body, he slid his hands down to stroke her clit, knowing that it would drive her to even bigger heights as they climaxed together.

Clint pounded into her again and again until he finally exploded inside of her. Their bodies were both covered in sweat, and when Lucy climbed off of him, she all but collapsed on the bed next to Clint.

"Mmmm," she purred into his ear. "You really are different than any other man. Most of them can never keep up with me."

Although Clint was still trying to catch his breath, he did manage to say, "I can see why. I'd be curious to see what you could do after a full night's sleep, when you've got all your strength."

Lucy snuggled up close to him, her naked curves fitting in perfectly to the contours of his body. "Well, you'd better get some shut-eye, because you're going to find out just what I'm capable of the moment you wake up tomorrow."

TWENTY-NINE

When the sun came up the next morning, it barely managed to shine through the clouds that were left over from the storm front that had passed through the night before. Dark gray clouds trailed behind the thunderheads like smoke that lingered in the path of a steam engine. The streets were still soft and messy, but at least the mud had dried to a thicker state than the dirty rivers that had flowed throughout all of Random.

Most of the locals were glad to see that the rain had finally stopped falling on their heads, but when they passed by the Rosewood, it seemed as though a black cloud was still hanging firmly in place. Several armed men circled the saloon like a band of soldiers guarding a fort. Inside, the place had been all but swept clean of anyone but the men who worked in Alonzo Bittermeyer's inner circle.

The boss himself paced across the large room from bar to fireplace, his hands clasped behind his back and a fire burning brightly in his eyes.

"Let's hear it, Connor," Bittermeyer snarled. "And believe me when I tell you that you'd best have good news for me."

The slender gunman was still wearing the same clothes as the night before. One look at the dark circles beneath his sunken eyes was more than enough to confirm the fact that his head hadn't touched a pillow in at least twenty-four hours. "I had a talk with a few of my people," Connor said. "And they say they spotted a new face headed toward the cabins used by your workers."

Bittermeyer's face darkened and he stopped dead in his tracks. "The ones right behind this place? How come I wasn't told about this earlier?"

Paul was there as well. And though he'd been up for just as long as Connor, he seemed none the worse for wear. "We had to confirm it before going off half-cocked. Jumping into a fight too soon," he added while turning to look at Stanton, who sat at one of the nearby tables, "can get a man shot up in a hurry."

As much as Stanton wanted to reply, he couldn't get off much more than a grunt. Every inch of him was caked with dried mud and he seemed to have barely enough energy to hold his head up.

"So do you have enough information now?" Bittermeyer asked. "Or are you two planning on wasting more of my valuable time?"

Connor nodded. "We've got plenty."

"Good. Then you'll move in today. I also want to do some moving of my own. If this stranger is holed up in the housing I provided for my workers, then that means one of them is probably helping him. And if that's the case, that means it's high time for this town to be reminded who is in charge of things."

That brought a smile to Paul's face. When he looked over to Connor, he saw an expression that was quite different. The smaller man's eyes were filled with hunger rather than anticipation, which made his face appear more animal than human.

Paul turned back toward Bittermeyer as something else
flashed through his mind. "Oh, I almost forgot. One of
the girls at Gracie's spent some time with a fella from
Oklahoma City a week or so back."

Impatience radiated from Bittermeyer like heat waves
from a desert floor. "So?"

"Turns out the fella wasn't just a fella. He was a U.S.
marshal sent to come looking for that deputy we buried
not too long ago."

"I see. And how long have you been sitting on that
particular fact?"

"About twenty minutes. She was going to tell me last
night, but she was . . . nervous. She only just got her nerve
up to come to me when I stopped by there to change my
clothes."

Bittermeyer scratched his chin and stepped up to the
large fireplace in the middle of the room. He swept up
one of the pokers with a casual hand and prodded some
of the smoldering coals. Twisting the iron and leaning in
to stab one of the thick logs that kept the flames going,
he thought to himself before spinning around with the
glowing steel in his fist.

"Perfect," he said while swinging the iron in a quick
half circle. "This is just perfect. The timing couldn't have
been better. Now I can set everything straight in the next
couple of days. As soon as I put the folks in this piss-
hole town back in line and rid myself of this stranger
who's been such a pain in my ass, I'll be ready to greet
this lawman. In fact, I might just put that one on display
for a month or two. Once he starts to rot, he'll make sure
that nobody dares to speak so much as a word against
me." Grinning widely, he added, "It'll be nice to have the
law working for me for a change."

Connor and Paul took a few steps back to keep out of
the reach of the hot poker, but didn't say a word. They
both knew when to put in their say in a conversation with

their boss and when to keep their mouths shut. This time was most definitely one of the latter.

Stanton watched all of this as well. His tired eyes took in his boss's rantings with growing disbelief. And for the first time since he'd started working for the man, he started to wonder if Bittermeyer might not only be power hungry, but completely insane as well.

THIRTY

Twisting on the balls of his feet, Bittermeyer reared back his arm and swung the iron until the hook on its side dug deep into the pile of wood at the base of the fireplace. The searing metal hissed when it made contact with the split piece of log, and a thin wisp of smoke curled up into the air.

"Here's the way it's going to work," Bittermeyer stated, his eyes burning almost as bright as the tip of the poker he'd been holding. "Connor and Paul, I want you two to flush out that stranger by putting the torch to a few of those houses I paid for."

"What about the folks inside?" Paul asked without showing a bit of concern for the people in question.

"To hell with them," Bittermeyer spat. "I bought those places and I can burn them down. If they're too stupid to clear out before their asses catch on fire, that ain't my concern. Just make sure they all see who's doing the burning. That way, they'll all know to come to me for an explanation."

Connor nodded. "And the stranger? You want us to take him there or bring him to you?"

"Doesn't matter. If possible, I'd like to deliver the final shot myself . . . and I will pay extra for such a pleasure. But if that can't happen, I'll settle on having the body brought here. I'm sure I can think of a good place to set it on display to discourage anyone else who decides to spit in the face of my hospitality."

Connor seemed more than pleased with that response. His eyes glazed over momentarily, as if he was already picturing what he would do with the bonus that had just been dangled in front of him.

Walking over to where Stanton was sitting, Bittermeyer slapped the flat of his hand against the table, which brought the local man leaping to his feet. "I want you to gather up the rest of your friends . . . the ones that want positions with my crew . . . and bring them here. I don't care who they are or what qualifications they have, so long as they can hold a gun or even an axe handle, have them come here because I'll be putting them all to work."

"Ex-excuse me, sir?" Stanton said while shaking his head.

"Gather up as many as you can find," Bittermeyer repeated excitedly. "I'll pay them all well enough. Just bring them here and arm them all. You know where to find the supplies you need. If my own workers are hiding the likes of this stranger, then that means the rest of the town is in even worse condition."

Bittermeyer turned to face all of his men and raised his voice to a pitch that boomed throughout the entire saloon. "I've been itching for a chance to clean out this town once and for all of anyone who doesn't appreciate what an easy life I give them. And the best way to do that is to show them just how bad they could possibly have it without being in my good graces. I don't care if we burn down half this town, I want my point to be made. By the time this day is through, I'll know that my enemies are dead and the rest will be too scared to lift a finger against me

ever again! They love this stranger so much, then they'll
all get to meet him face-to-face after I nail his carcass to
the front of this bar."

Connor and Paul were beaming as though they were
gazing proudly upon the face of a beloved father. Their
hands were already drifting to their weapons in anticipation of what the day would bring.

Stanton, on the other hand, didn't seem quite so eager.
"Sir, isn't this just a bit . . ." He pinched off his question
the instant he saw Bittermeyer turn to lock him with a
fiery stare.

"A bit too what?" Bittermeyer asked. "You don't know
what it took for me to get control of this town, and you
sure as hell don't know what it takes to keep it. If you'd
like to get a better idea, then perhaps I should take you
to the spot outside of town where we planted the lawmen
that tried to set up shop here in Random. If you think
there was just that one, then you'd be sadly mistaken.

"Then again," he said while turning to look at Paul,
"we won't have to do that after all, will we?"

Paul's dark eyes smoldered with intensity as he slowly
shook his head. "No, sir. Not at all. We should have another live example riding into town any time now. In fact,
there should be at least two or three of them."

"Ahh," Bittermeyer said with a grin. "Variety. Maybe
I'll ride them through town strung up like scarecrows.
That should keep the rest in line. And the next time they
hear about one of the law coming to Random, they'll either come running to me or do their damndest to make
sure to discourage them deputies any way they can."

Finally, Bittermeyer let his voice quiet down to a rumbling baritone. He took a few deep breaths and strode to
the front window, where he stood looking out like a be-
nevolent ruler surveying his kingdom. "I'm sick to death
of being unappreciated in this place that I created. Last
night, that stranger taught me just how far I've let this

town as well as my own men slip. I want to thank him for that. Do you understand me, Paul? Connor? I want to thank him."

Bittermeyer's hand flashed to his shoulder holster and drew the silver-handled Smith & Wesson revolver stored there. His motion was quick as a blink, and in another blink the pistol had spun twice around his finger and was back in leather.

"I should have done this a long time ago," Bittermeyer continued in an almost nostalgic tone. "Remember when we first rolled into this town?"

"Yes, sir," Paul and Connor said as one.

Taking in one more deep breath, Bittermeyer closed his eyes and touched his fingertips to the glass. After letting out a slow exhale which caused a circle of fog to form in front of his face, he said, "I can still see it. The look in these folks' eyes when we took over and showed them that the only law they needed was *our* law. They looked at us with respect. They looked at us with fear."

That last word struck a chord with both of the more experienced gunmen. It did with Stanton as well, but a chord that resonated deep inside of him and shook him all the way down to the bone.

"The fear used to be thick in this town," Bittermeyer said fondly. "It used to force them to pay what they owed us and not ask any questions. I used to be able to walk outside, lift my nose to the wind and smell that fear at any time of day." Turning to Connor and Paul, he added, "They're not afraid anymore, boys. But you know something? They will be.

"After tonight, they'll all be too scared to bury their dead and we'll finally get the respect that we so truly deserve."

THIRTY-ONE

Clint woke the next morning well after sunrise. Even though he hadn't gotten much rest considering all he'd been through the night before, his muscles still seemed ready to go and his blood pumped quickly through his veins.

He did his best not to wake Lucy as he slipped out of her bed. As much as he'd enjoyed their lovemaking before, he didn't want to press his luck by rousing her for the early morning session she'd promised him. Besides, she looked beautiful asleep with half her body covered by the sheets. Her pale, creamy skin nearly blended in with the linens, giving her an almost dreamlike appearance that made Clint struggle to keep himself from crawling back in beside her. Lucy's red hair spilled over her face and across the pillow in stark contrast to the cool paleness of the rest of her body.

Clint's spirits were heightened even more when he actually managed to catch a glimpse of the sun as he took his first look out the window. It wasn't much, but the few rays that managed to break through the passing cloud cover were a sight for weary eyes, and before he knew it, Clint was dressed and through the door so he could feel the touch of the sun against his skin before he forgot it completely.

He was still buttoning his shirt when he saw some commotion coming from the end of the row of houses. There was a group of around a dozen people chattering excitedly about something that caused several of them to go running off toward their homes.

After making his way toward the group, Clint tried to catch what was being said. The instant he was spotted by the others, however, all the chatter stopped and a heavy silence fell over the gathering.

"I didn't mean to intrude," Clint said while glancing around at all the faces turned in his direction. "But I just heard the commotion and thought I'd see what's going on. If it's a private matter, then I can—"

"You can get the hell out of here," one of the local women snapped.

Clint flinched back as though the words had reached out and slapped him across the face. "Pardon me?"

Another of the women stepped forward. A man at her side reached out to take hold of her by the elbow, but the woman jerked free and marched up to within a couple feet of where Clint was standing. "You heard her," she seethed. "Haven't you caused enough trouble? We were all doing just fine before you got here and now . . . now we'll all . . ." She couldn't say another thing once she broke down into a fit of sobs and was forced to bury her face in her hands.

"Hush up, Margaret," the man beside her said. "I heard he's just as bad as any of the others."

Clint looked around for any explanation of what was going on. Even a hint as to where he should look would have been appreciated, but all he got for his efforts were a whole lot of angry stares or faces that were averted from him altogether.

"Could someone tell me what this is all about?" he asked once he saw that no other help would be forthcoming.

For a moment, nobody seemed willing to talk to him. When he started to address people directly, they either turned away or stepped back as though they were trying not to get hit by an incoming fist. That was when Clint realized what was running through the crowd.

Fear.

They were all not only deathly afraid, but they were afraid of *him*.

Clint forced himself to wipe away anything in his appearance that might give the wrong impression. His eyes instinctively found the guns on several of the men's hips and he knew that fear was one of the first things that might cause some of those guns to be drawn. And once that happened, there would be no turning back.

"Look," he said while holding his empty hands in front of him, "I don't know what's going on here, but whatever it is, I've got nothing to do with it."

One of the men at the back of the group stepped forward, his hand resting on the grip of his gun. Close-cropped, light brown hair covered his scalp and a bushy mustache covered his upper lip. He was dressed in simple coveralls and boots that looked like they were held together by nothing more than the high hopes of their wearer. "You've done enough, mister. Just do us a favor and get the hell out of town before it starts burning down around your ears."

Despite what the man said, Clint couldn't detect any threat in his voice. That didn't, however, answer any of the questions racing through his mind.

"What do you mean?" Clint asked. "What's happened?"

The first woman who'd spoken looked between Clint and the other man. "Why don't you go ahead and tell him,

Jed? He wants to know what he started, then go ahead and tell him."

Clint stepped forward and stood as passively as possible. "Sure, Jed. Go on and tell me."

"Mr. Bittermeyer's given us warning. We need to send you to him before his men come looking. 'Cause when they do, they'll be finishing what they already started."

In response to Clint's expression, Jed motioned for the group to part. Once that happened, Clint could see past the people and to the end of the street, where one of the quaint little homes stood without a ceiling. The three remaining walls were blackened and leaning precariously to one side.

"There," Jed said. "That's what they started. The only reason they stopped was to tell us what I just told you."

Clint couldn't take his eyes away from the charred remains of the house. The building hadn't been much, but it had been somebody's home. Now it was a scorched shell. "Was anybody hurt?" he asked.

Several of the women started to cry and Jed steeled himself by clenching his jaw. "Two young'uns were inside when the fire started. We put out the flames before too long, but one of 'em doesn't look good. He's at the doc's right now."

The first question on Clint's mind was why he hadn't heard the fire or any of the efforts to put it out. But when he took another look at the similar homes, he saw that they were mostly constructed of old timber and crumbling brick. The parts that could have burned would have done so real quickly. The rest would have simply fallen down in a pile . . . much like what he was looking at just then.

"It burned down before we knew what was happening," Jed explained. "The ones that started it saw to that."

Clint was so mad he could barely think straight. "How long before they said they'd come back?"

"Two hours."

"Take your families out of here right now."

"But this is our home! We can't just—"

"I said now!" Clint shouted.

Jed and several of the other men stepped forward as if to face Clint down. But when they saw that Clint's eyes were focused on something else completely, they turned to look at what it was that he'd seen. When they were all looking at the same spot, their eyes grew wide and the women started to scream.

The torches in the hands of the men that were walking toward the houses burned like hellfire in the damp morning breeze. They walked in two rows of five men each. Black smoke rose from the flames to mark the men's trail with a dark smudge in the air over their heads. As soon as they got close to the first house, one of the men separated from the rest and lowered his torch so that it was level with a small square window.

Jed turned back to look at Clint, but could find no trace of him. "Jesus Christ," he whispered as panic took hold of his heart and mind. When he looked for Clint again, he found him . . . stepping out of Lucy's home, clinching his gun belt around his waist.

THIRTY-TWO

Lucy hadn't been in bed when Clint went back to get his gun. More than that, she hadn't been in the house at all. Since he didn't have much time to think about where she'd gone, Clint took his Colt from where he'd left it and hoped that she'd seen enough to know that it was no longer safe to be around here.

At least, not for the moment anyway.

The buckle snapped into place and the gun belt settled perfectly into its familiar spot around Clint's waist. The weight of the specially modified Colt felt like a familiar part of Clint's body. The leather was so worn that it moved easily with every step he took, conforming to him after years of serving Clint so well.

When he stepped back outside, Clint saw the group of locals just starting to scatter. The one named Jed spotted him immediately and couldn't decide whether or not he should be happy about Clint's arrival.

All Clint cared about was that Jed moved along with all the others. He was glad when he saw Jed along with the rest of the group clear the street and race toward their homes.

"That's it," shouted the man at the head of the torch-bearers. "Go on and run. Mr. Bittermeyer don't take to no ingrates livin' in his town. And he won't tolerate no traitors on his payroll!"

Looking over to the one who stood ready to burn another house, the leader nodded once and said, "Light it up! As for the rest of ya," he said to the men behind him, "pick a place and let's get started. And be ready for that stranger. He should be—"

A single shot rang through the air, cracking loudly over the sound of feet on mud and snapping flames.

Every one of the torchbearers wheeled to face Clint, their eyes picking him out as the flow of rushing locals thinned out to leave him alone in the middle of the street. Clint's bullet whipped through the air and drilled through the torch that was just about to be sent through the window of one house. The burning piece of wood spun away from the man who'd been holding it and hissed loudly as it landed in a puddle of standing rainwater.

"I'm right here," Clint said to the man in front of Bittermeyer's thugs. "And the next one of you that steps near one of those houses with a torch gets blown clean out of his boots."

The warning hung in the air like the black clouds that had rolled through town the night before.

The man at the head of the group fixed a pair of narrow, beady eyes upon Clint. "So you'd be the one that killed Maher and Kade?"

Shrugging, Clint said, "That's hard to say. I didn't get a chance to catch their names before they started trying to put a bullet into me."

"Mr. Bittermeyer has some words for you."

"I can think of a few for him as well, but I'd rather not say them with women and children about."

Shifting his torch from one hand to another, the man took another step forward and reached for the holster strapped to his side. He stopped less than a second later when he saw the flicker of motion that was Clint's own gun being brought around to cover him.

"You're outgunned, stranger," the leader said. "If you come quietly, we can take you to see Mr. Bittermeyer and then you can get the hell out of Random while you can still draw a breath."

"Sure. I'll come with you so the rest of your men can put the torch to these people's homes? I don't think so."

The smug grin on the leader's face quickly melted away. Taking a quick glance over each shoulder to make sure he still had his group behind him, he stepped back and pointed to the man who still stood in front of the first house. That one's torch still sputtered and hissed in the puddle near his feet.

"Someone relight Ben's torch." When he saw Clint move again, the leader shifted his gaze that way. "If you don't come with us right now, we'll toss our fire at any building we can reach. And when they start burning down, it'll be on your head."

"That's where the problem is," Clint said calmly. "Your boss has already tipped his hand. He's a back-shooting coward who needs to hide behind a small army to feel like a real man. I don't know all of what's going on in this town, but whatever it is, it's about to stop. And if you think I believe for one second that it'll stop once I hand myself over to you, then you must think I'm even dumber than all of you put together."

"Then we got no choice, mister."

"On the contrary, you've got two choices: put your torches out and leave . . . or die."

THIRTY-THREE

Despite the fact that the torchbearers outnumbered Clint ten to one, there wasn't a man among them who seemed all too anxious to be the first one to attack him. Instead, they looked to the one acting as their leader and waited to see what he was about to do.

The leader started to take a step forward, but stopped himself at the last moment and tried to pass off the motion as a shifting of his feet. "You can't be that stupid, mister. We could cut you down and still burn this place in no time at all."

"You think so?" Clint replied. "Then perhaps you'd like to be the first one to try."

Every second that passed caused the doubt in some of the men's eyes to grow. The others looked to their leader with increasing agitation. Either way, it was obvious that if something was going to happen, it would happen real soon.

The leader let his arm fall down low at his side. Turning as if to look toward the men behind him, he quickly shifted on his feet and made a desperate grab for his side arm. "Take him!" was all he said before his words along with the quietness in the air were blasted away by gunfire.

Clint hadn't taken his eyes off the front man for even a fraction of a second. The moment the leader made his move, Clint was already starting to make his as well. His hand became a blur of motion, and when it came up to hip level, the modified Colt was spitting out a tongue of sparks and smoke.

As promised, the leader of the arsonists was the first to drop. Clint's bullet drilled a messy hole through the center of his chest and sent him flying a few feet backward. Although he'd been starting to throw his torch toward one of the nearby homes, the leader didn't even have enough strength to pitch it halfway, and the burning wood landed in a nearby puddle of mud.

Of the nine remaining men, four of them had managed to draw and start firing while the others were either bolting for cover or still trying to clear leather. Two of the ones doing the shooting dropped to one knee, demonstrating at least a bit of levelheadedness under fire.

Although Clint's instincts were to throw himself toward a nearby water trough before one of the other men got a lucky shot, he steeled himself and held his position for another couple of seconds. Even for one as used to being shot at as he, those two seconds were some of the longest ones he could imagine.

Clint's main concern was to thin out the group's numbers. Even before their leader hit the ground, Clint was already picking his next target and taking aim. The next man in his sights was the first one he could see who seemed to be pointing his pistol in the right direction, and after a moment's concentration followed by a squeeze of his trigger, Clint sent that one spinning off his feet, a crimson spray forming behind his head.

The bullets were whipping through the air in a swarm that grew thicker with each passing moment. Clint knew it would be suicide to stay in the middle of it much longer, but he held his ground, turned to the side and dropped to one knee to give the others a much smaller target.

Adjusting his aim from his new position, Clint sighted down the Colt's barrel as if he was pointing at one of the torch-bearing figures. As he locked eyes with that one, the other man's rifle sent out a plume of smoke half a second before Clint fired. The moment he felt the Colt buck in his hand, Clint pushed off with the boot that was against the ground and launched himself into a sideways roll, which carried him toward the trough he'd spotted before.

As he moved, Clint could hear the other man grunt in pain, but it was impossible for him to know right away whether or not he'd taken him out completely. Clint heard some of the gunfire thinning out as he reached the trough. Pulling his feet beneath him and getting into a crouch, Clint chanced a look toward the torchbearers and saw his most recent target struggling to get to his feet while clutching at his side. That one was still moving, but he didn't look ready to fire right away.

All around, Clint could hear the sounds of panic. Frightened cries of women and children flowed around the stomping of scurrying feet, soon to be followed by the dreaded crackle of flames. Cursing under his breath, Clint forced himself to stay focused on his top priority, which was dealing with the men trying to fill him full of holes.

Sporadic gunshots came from all around as some of the torchbearers who'd run for cover finally got enough courage to start firing their weapons. From what Clint could hear, most of them had pistols. There were a few distinct cracks of rifles, as well as the occasional shotgun's roar. With every passing second, the line of fire tightened in closer to Clint's position, letting him know that his cover wouldn't be worth much of anything before too long.

Clint poked his head around the side of the trough and immediately spotted a pair of men creeping toward him, each with a gun in one hand and a torch in the other.

Reflexively, he brought the Colt up to bear and squeezed the trigger twice in quick succession, doing his best to put a round into each man before ducking back behind the wooden trough.

One of the men cried out in pain, his voice quickly changing into a wet gurgle before being chocked off altogether. A second voice launched a stream of obscenities in Clint's direction, which was quickly followed by the thump of something heavy hitting the muddy ground.

Clint's fingers raced through the motions of dumping out his spent cartridges and replacing them with fresh ones pulled from his gun belt. As he reloaded the Colt, he took another quick look around the trough, just as the smell of burning wood drifted into his nostrils.

His first fear was that some of the houses were already catching on fire. Although his fears were put at ease in that respect fairly quickly, a whole new set of worries raced through his mind when he got a look at what was going on.

The first thing he saw when he took his quick glance was, indeed, flames, but they were not coming from any of the houses that he could see. Instead, they were coming from the front of the trough he'd been using for cover. Lying on the ground, one of Bittermeyer's men held a torch to the trough, a leering smile sliding onto his face as the flames began to come to life.

"He's comin', boys," the man with the torch shouted without taking his eyes from Clint. "I flushed him out for ya!"

Clint snapped the Colt's cylinder shut with a flick of his wrist. Taking a quick look around, he couldn't spot a single place he could use for cover that wouldn't force him to run through yards of open space. Voices began closing in around him as footsteps rushed forward, the gunfire tapering off as the remaining torchbearers waited for their next clear shot.

Only a few seconds had elapsed, but already black smoke was billowing from the trough and flowing over Clint's face. He knew if he stayed there much longer, he would either pass out from the smoke or be torn apart by bullets the moment the trough collapsed in front of him.

Clint's only remaining choice was to make a run for cover. And the only path to cover would send him into the sights of at least six anxious trigger fingers.

Suddenly, a vague glimmer of hope drifted through Clint's mind. Gathering himself into a coiled mass, he tightened his grip on the modified Colt and prepared to move. Since every one of the gunmen was ready for him to break from cover, he would gain at least a small bit of surprise by running in the one direction they might not be expecting . . .

. . . right down their throats.

THIRTY-FOUR

The tall, heavyset gunman had been one of the few Bittermeyer hired that actually had some experience under fire. Most of the other boys were just that: boys with no more than a firearm and the youthful anxiousness to use it. Ben had done his best to train them whenever he could, and now that the lead was starting to fly, they were all looking to him as the man to replace their fallen leader.

As soon as he heard that the stranger had been flushed from his hiding spot, Ben smelled that something just wasn't quite right. The stranger was too good, he moved with too much experience, to be routed so easily.

What gave Ben an even more disturbing feeling in the pit of his stomach was the way all the other boys reacted to the shouted words.

"Let's get him!" one of them yelled.

"Take him down!"

Those words were followed by a series of excited whoops and hollers, battle cries of those that didn't know any better.

Ben's first instinct was to hold them back, but they were too wrapped up in the moment, and before he even had a chance to get a single warning out, the stranger had already erupted from behind the burning trough like a round blazing from the end of a smoking barrel.

Most of the younger gunmen were running for the trough, firing their guns with every other step. The ones that were close enough had already focused their attention on the end farthest away from the fire, assuming that anyone trying to run would head away from the fire as well as the oncoming guns.

But that's not where the stranger emerged.

Instead, he popped up from the flames themselves. And though the difference was small, it was enough to throw off all but one of the remaining torchbearers, giving Clint a second or two of free time to use any way he saw fit.

Clint's first priority was to get closer to one of the houses so he could put something solid between himself and Bittermeyer's men. He saw immediately that his plan had bought him a few valuable seconds and would have given him more if not for the one figure that hadn't been tricked into looking the wrong way at the right time.

Ben stood his ground, remaining on one knee while sighting down the barrel of a Spencer rifle.

His eyes going immediately to the figure with the rifle, Clint ran as fast as his legs could carry him. With the blood pumping through his body and his heart slamming against the inside of his ribs, he still felt as though he was hardly moving at all.

Clint moved the Colt without having to divert any thought to the action. His arm moved as if it had a mind of its own and was fighting to keep the rest of him alive. Aiming from the hip, Clint twisted his body at the last possible second and pulled the trigger.

The Colt went off at the precise moment that the Spencer Ben was holding delivered its deadly cargo through the air.

The sound of the rifle's bullet was like an angry hornet hissing toward Clint's face. He couldn't tell where he'd hit the rifleman yet, but Clint wasn't about to waste even a sliver of time trying to find out. Instead, he rolled himself to one side, forcing himself toward the ground as though he'd twisted his ankle as he was plummeting to the earth.

As he fell, Clint felt a burning sensation tear through his chin on the left side. At first, it felt like any other scrape, but then his jaw started to throb as though he'd just gotten an uppercut from a heavyweight prizefighter. The pain grew as he dropped to the ground, and when he finally hit, Clint had to struggle to keep from losing consciousness.

For a second, the entire world almost stopped.

The sights and sounds going through Clint's mind became a blur of nonsense. His own body wasn't willing to respond to his brain's commands. And the more he fought to take back the reins, the more they slipped from his grasp.

Suddenly, there was a horrendous impact against Clint's entire right side as the ground slammed into him like a giant's club. The impact rattled him straight down to the bone, and although it sent waves of dull pain enough to every part of his body, the sensation was like a bucket of cold water splashed onto his face.

Clint did his best to roll with the fall as everything around him snapped back into normal speed.

When he came to a wobbly kneeling stance, Clint found Ben still watching him. The other man's rifle was coming around for a second shot. Even in his dazed state, Clint knew he had maybe half a second to act before the killing round would be speeding toward him.

Once again, Clint's only option was to cut straight to the meat of the fight, and he launched himself toward Ben with arms outstretched, a snarling battle cry issuing from the depths of his soul.

The first thing to hit was Clint's left fist against the barrel of Ben's rifle. As soon as his flesh touched metal, Clint felt the steel turn painfully hot as the Spencer's trigger was once again pulled. He was momentarily deafened by the gunshot, but Clint managed to brace himself against the pain enough to grab hold of the rifle and pull it from Ben's hands.

Searing hot pain sizzled Clint's flesh as he tightened his fingers around the Spencer. Every instinct in his mind and body screamed for him to let go of the hot steel, but he clenched his fist tighter, brought the weapon behind his head and swung it outward as though he was swinging an axe.

Ben's eyes became wide as saucers and his jaw dropped open as the butt of his own rifle slammed into the side of his face and knocked him over sideways. The rifleman was out before he hit the ground, unable to even get his arms up to brace himself for impact.

Clint knew better than to dwell on his small victory. Instead, he mentally cursed himself for taking so much time with one man while five others were setting out to burn down the homes of these innocent people. Thinking of those torches, Clint turned the pain in his hand and face into a powerful fuel that drove him to move even faster.

Spinning around on his heels, Clint flipped the Spencer rifle in the air, caught hold of it around the handle and slid his finger beneath the trigger guard. A weapon in each fist, Clint ran forward and charged into the firing line.

THIRTY-FIVE

Jed's first instinct was to make sure that his wife and neighbors were all right. Once he'd seen them off to safety, he quickly gathered up some of the other men who lived in the houses behind the Rosewood and took a quick head count.

"Where's everyone else?" he asked, looking at the half dozen men who huddled together behind one of the homes at the end of the row.

An older fellow by the name of William McCormick gestured wildly toward a small barn. "I had the missus bring them in there. They should be safe once they get the doors blocked up."

Jed nodded and watched as the women he'd been shepherding made their way to the barn. "That'll have to do. Now what are we going to do to help that stranger?"

"Help him?" William said. "He started this whole damn thing!"

Jed's body flinched forward as if to strike the older man, but he managed to stop himself at the last moment. "Are you blind? That stranger just took on ten men to try and keep our homes from burning to the ground. If you want to turn your back on him now, then that's your

137

choice. I only hope you find some way to look at yourself in a mirror someday."

Without waiting for a response, Jed turned and walked toward a woodpile near the back door of the house where they were gathered. He grabbed the thickest log he could wrap his fingers around and started walking toward the sound of fighting.

When he reached the corner of the house, he heard footsteps coming up behind him. Jed took a quick look over his shoulder and found not one, but every one of the other men standing there grasping wooden clubs similar to the one Jed himself was wielding.

At the front of the group was William, who kept his chin held high and the piece of timber hefted over his shoulder. "When you're right, you're right," he said. "So what do we do now?"

Jed slapped the older man on the shoulder and peeked around the corner. "Near as I can tell, the stranger already took out a good bunch of them. There's still plenty left, though."

Leaning out to get a better look at the surrounding homes, Jed quickly pulled himself back. "The fire," he said while all the color seemed to drain from his face. "It's spreading down the line."

None of the men asked which houses were ablaze. Instead, they set their features firmly and started moving around the house. Jed quickly pointed out the gunmen he'd sighted and took a breath as they emerged into the firefight.

At first, the scene was nothing more than a mess of chaos and swirling black smoke. Soon, however, Jed and his neighbors were able to pick out several faces that they recognized as belonging to Bittermeyer's crew. Gunshots blasted through the air and flames crackled on either side, but none of this seemed to concern the men too much, as the sight of their burning community spurred them toward the torchbearers.

None of the gunmen seemed to notice the locals until one of them nearly ran over William like a freight train. "What the hell?" the gunman said as he wheeled around to get a look at what had almost sent him to the dirt.

Just as he got a look at William's face, the gunman caught sight of something flying toward him from the corner of his eye. Jed's crude weapon smashed into the gunman's skull, snapping his head to one side.

Already clutching a pistol, the gunman tried to bring up his weapon, but was unable to do so before Jed's second swing connected with his left temple. There was a burst of pain and then total blackness as the gunman dropped over like a sack of rocks.

The neighbors emerged in a rush, preparing themselves for the next gunman to come their way. Instead, they were greeted by a wave of flames as an adjacent home was put to the torch. Jed managed to focus on where most of the gunfire was concentrated and picked out several shapes converging on what looked to be a solitary figure.

"I see him," Jed reported to the men directly behind him. "Some of you need to start putting out these flames. You three," he said while pointing to a row of thick-necked young men who'd worked their muscles up after years of manual labor, "come with me."

William pushed in front of one of the bigger men until he was standing next to Jed. "Me too. I want to help."

"I ain't got time to argue, Will. Just be sure to keep your head down."

With that, Jed and his makeshift posse rushed toward the group of gunmen while the remaining neighbors began tending to the burning buildings.

On their way toward the gun battle, Jed came across a trough that had been set on fire. Lying there on his side was one of Bittermeyer's men, struggling to take aim with an Army model pistol. The man was moving slowly, and was just thumbing back the weapon's hammer when Jed ran up to him.

The wounded gunman cocked his pistol, lined Clint up squarely in his sights and then felt the dull, throbbing pain of a split log crashing into the back of his skull. The back of his pistol rushed up to meet him as his face was driven forward, pulling the barrel upward as his finger reflexively jerked against the trigger.

Hearing the shot, Jed thought he might have been hit before he could do any good for the stranger that had tried to save him and his family. The gunman's arm was cocked back, frozen in position before Jed had been able to make his swing.

But even though the killer's gun had gone off, Jed wasn't even harmed. That was when he saw the gunman slump to one side, the entire back of his head glistening with blood. Standing over the unconscious figure, William hefted his piece of timber in one hand, preparing himself to take another swing.

"Much obliged, old-timer," Jed said with an offhanded wave.

William stared down at the prone figure between his feet and let out the breath he'd been holding. "He was . . . I saw . . ." Taking a moment to compose himself, the older man kicked the pistol away from the gunman's hand.

None of the small group of friends and neighbors said another word. Instead, they simply steeled themselves against the danger ahead . . . and moved on.

THIRTY-SIX

The instant Clint turned on the approaching gunmen, he was already firing both of the guns in his possession. The report of the Spencer rifle mixed in with the familiar bark of the Colt as he leveled the guns at the first targets he could find.

One of Bittermeyer's men was firing as quickly as he could. Gripping a revolver in one hand, he fanned the hammer with his other palm to create a spray of lead that worked its way closer to where Clint was standing. Before he could pull the weapon on target, he was taken off his feet by a piece of hot lead that had been spit out by Clint's Colt.

As soon as he saw that figure drop, Clint turned his attention to the next one in line. From the corner of his eye, he spotted yet another torchbearer making a dash for one of the houses which hadn't been touched by flames. Clint snapped out the lever of his commandeered rifle and spun the weapon in a tight circle, which ejected the spent cartridge, and shoved a new one into place. Taking half a second to aim, Clint brought the rifle around and pulled the trigger, dropping the man with the torch less than five feet away from the house he'd been intending to burn.

Although there were still shots being fired around him, Clint could tell that the amount had dwindled considerably. It had been second nature to keep tabs on the remaining gunmen in the back of his mind, but as Clint looked around, he realized he was coming up one or two short.

Just then, he spotted a few figures running toward him with their bodies stooped over in a low crouch. Clint's first impulse was to take a shot at them, but he quickly saw that they were holding neither guns nor torches, but thick pieces of wood. When they got a little closer, their faces started registering in Clint's mind.

He couldn't think of any of their names at the moment, but Clint knew that the approaching men were the ones that lived in the surrounding homes.

"Get down!" Clint hollered.

Not all of them were sharp enough to react too quickly, but several of them stooped down a little lower as some of the gunfire was turned toward them instead of Clint. This also allowed Clint to spot a muzzle flash from one of the gunmen who'd been shooting from behind the door of one of the nearby homes.

The gunman had thrown open the door and was standing behind the thick wood, leaning out to take the occasional shot before ducking back into hiding. Up until now, Clint hadn't been able to spot this shooter and had just managed to keep himself covered through random shots in every direction. Now that he'd gotten a look at the gunman, Clint thought of a way to take the man out.

But first, he had to keep anyone else from stepping into the path of a bullet.

"What the hell are you doing?" Clint asked as he rushed toward the approaching locals.

Jed pulled William by the front of his shirt, all but tossing the old man into the mud. "We wanted to help before you got hurt." Wincing, he added, "I hope we're not too late."

Reaching up to the nasty-looking wound on his chin, Clint wiped away some blood and flicked it off his fingers. "This isn't as bad as it looks. You need to worry about these fires. Go get some help and gather up some water, but leave these men to me. I don't need you men getting yourselves hurt."

Another set of gunshots whipped through the air. The only good thing about the fires roaring on all sides was the fact that the smoke being produced served to obscure the gunmen's aim and provide Clint with thick, swirling cover.

"I ain't leaving you," Jed insisted. "We can help. We've already helped."

Clint looked over the desperate men and noted the thick coating of blood on the ends of some of the clubs they held. "Yeah," he said. "I'm sure you can help. How much help have you given me, by the way?"

"Two," William said proudly. "We knocked two of 'em straight on their asses."

More shots hissed in the air, punching through the smoky curtain and drawing closer to Clint and the others.

"Taking out two of them is more than enough," Clint said, his muscles twitching in anticipation of his next move. "But you got lucky, plain and simple. Go find some cover before that luck runs out."

Rather than argue one second longer, Clint spun the rifle with a sharp snap of his wrist and chambered the next round. He then fired a shot from the Colt to cover himself as he stepped into the veil of smoke separating him from the rest of Bittermeyer's torchbearers.

THIRTY-SEVEN

Behind him, Clint could hear the footsteps of the local men and could only hope that they were taking his advice and not doing something that might put their lives in even greater danger than they already were. Clint knew his time was running out. Either more men were going to come rushing out of Bittermeyer's saloon or he would get blown out of his boots by one of the shooters already present.

It was only a matter of time before one of these shooters took Clint down either through luck or persistence. Whichever it was, Clint knew he'd be just as dead. That meant his best chance for getting out of there alive was to end this fight *now*.

The moment he stepped through the smoke, Clint saw what was waiting for him on the other side. One of the gunmen was standing about twenty yards away, apparently caught right as he was set to charge toward Clint in one final rush. The other was still seeking cover behind a thick front door, poking his head out just now to take another shot.

Both of the gunmen acted simultaneously, raising their arms as soon as they caught sight of their target. Clint's mind was working much faster, however, and his reflexes were so much sharper after years of grinding them to a razor's edge.

Keeping his eyes trained at a spot between both of the gunmen, Clint lifted the rifle to greet the man to his left, who stood in the open. One squeeze of the trigger sent that one snapping back as hot lead chewed through his upper body.

Less than half a second after that, Clint aimed his Colt for a spot on the door that the last man was using as a shield. The round slammed into the thick wood, gouging a deep pit through the sturdy lumber and causing the man behind it to pull back reflexively before getting a chance to fire again.

Clint kept on walking slowly forward. He saw the first gunman's body relax and knew that he'd put that one down for good. Therefore, he turned his attention to the last one, who was still hiding and waiting for another chance.

Certain that the gunman wouldn't wait in his spot forever, Clint spun the rifle around his hand, which levered in the next round. As soon as his fingers closed around the handle, he held the rifle ready and lifted the Colt.

The sixth round from his pistol tore through the air, punching into the same spot as the previous bullet, which managed to carve a shallow hole through the thick, weathered door.

After planting his feet, Clint dropped the Colt into its holster and took up the rifle with both hands. He made sure there was a live cartridge in the chamber, sighted carefully down the barrel and said, "Be smarter than the rest. Toss out that gun and torch so I can take you in."

A dull, flickering orange glow showed through the window of the house. The motion of the light made it possible for Clint to guess where the torch was going even though its bearer was still cowering behind his cover. That light stayed put for a second, but quickly began to move to one side, causing the lace curtains in the window to burst into flames.

"Go to hell!" the gunman shouted as his pistol and the smallest sliver of his face became visible from behind the door.

Clint exhaled calmly, made a slight adjustment in his aim and squeezed the trigger. The rifle made a sound similar to a loud pop and kicked against Clint's shoulder. Its bullet spun through the smoky air, passed neatly through the hole created by the Colt and buried itself into the gunman's body.

Knowing that the first two shots, fired by the Colt, would have passed by the gunman while he was huddling for cover, Clint also knew that another bullet going through that same hole would strike home once the gunman was closer to the door's edge. His theory proved correct once the gunman stumbled forward into view and pitched face-first onto the porch.

Clint ran up to the last two bodies and checked them over up close. "It's all right," he called out once he was certain the fight, if not the life, had gone out of Bittermeyer's men.

First, Jed, William and the men with them came running forward. Then, neighbors began streaming out from where they'd been hiding, turning their attention almost immediately to their burning homes. By the time Clint got back to his feet, he saw dozens of others come running from the opposite direction, their hands filled with buckets of water.

Clint's first impulse was to charge toward the Rosewood so he could cut off any other attack before Bittermeyer sent it. But then he saw that his presence was needed right where he was. The bitter smell of smoke and the taste of ash at the back of his throat told him to stay and help while he could, at least until the fires had been brought somewhat under control.

Tossing the rifle to the ground, Clint stepped into a line of men passing buckets of water toward one of the houses most engulfed by flames. All around him, some of the smaller fires were put out before they could spread to the houses at the back of the row.

After an hour or so, Clint was relieved by one of the young men who'd been ready to fight at Jed and William's side. Before he could move on to another fire, Clint felt a hand close around his elbow.

It was Jed. The man's face was covered with grit and sweat, but his eyes seemed alive and vital. "You've done more than enough for us, mister. Why don't you get some rest before you fall over? Lord knows you've earned it."

"There's more that needs doing," Clint replied. "That is . . . unless you still need an extra hand around here."

Jed looked around proudly. "Looks like we're only going to lose one house, but the rest of the fires should be out before they do too much damage. My thanks to you, mister. The only reason this whole street ain't burning is because you kept more of those bastards from lighting it up."

Clint shook his head and took in the sight of the occasional flame crackling within a thick haze of black smoke. "This isn't over," he said, more to himself than anyone around him. "But it will be soon."

Glancing around at his neighborhood, Jed wiped away some of the sweat that had trickled into his eyes. "You don't have to do any more. You don't have to get yourself killed. Hell, we don't even know your name." But when he turned around to get an answer from the man who'd saved his community from total destruction, Jed found that the man had already gone.

The solitary figure was walking through the smoke and toward the Rosewood saloon.

THIRTY-EIGHT

Standing inside his small, yet lavishly decorated office, Alonzo Bittermeyer clasped his hands behind his back and watched the frenzied activity going on behind his saloon. One by one, the fires that he'd paid to start were being put out by the people whom he'd considered for so long to be nothing more than a commodity.

"Look at them," he said. "They run about like ants and you know who they are?"

Behind him, there was the subtle sound of a troubled breath being taken and then a vaguely trembling voice. ". . . Who are they, Alonzo?"

"They, my dear, are the workers that make their living from the salaries that I pay them. They are *my* workers and the only reason they live is because I allow them to." Spinning around on his heels, Bittermeyer looked out through eyes narrowed with rage. "I put the food on their tables! I built the roofs over their goddamn heads! And they repay me by spitting in my face? Killing my own men?"

Bittermeyer slammed his fist down upon his desk, causing gold-plated pens and velvet blotters to jump like scolded dogs. The plush carpeting and finely papered walls seemed to hold onto his voice for as long as they could before Bittermeyer's rage finally faded away into uncomfortable silence.

There were only two other chairs in the room besides the one behind the mahogany desk. Both were elegantly carved and padded with thick, expensive materials. But no matter how comfortable the chair was, it was unable to calm the mind of the person sitting in it.

Doing her best to keep from showing just how nervous she was, Lucy crossed her legs and folded her hands upon her knee. Her green eyes twitched between Bittermeyer and his gold pen set, unable to remain on one but feeling oddly comforted by the other.

"Look at me," Bittermeyer commanded with a snap of his fingers. "Or do you think I'm screaming just to hear the sound of my own voice?"

The light of the room seemed to converge upon those gold-plated trinkets. In fact, as silly as it might have sounded to anyone else, Lucy thought those pens were the only things that looked even vaguely warm in the entire room. Everything else, from the furniture to the cruel man behind it, was colder than the bottom of a frozen lake.

As much as she didn't want to, Lucy managed to pull her eyes away from the glitter of gold and look into Bittermeyer's expectant eyes. She did this partially out of a knee-jerk response to the barked command and partly from the jab she felt at the back of her head from Stanton, who was positioned directly behind her.

"That's better," Bittermeyer said. "Now, do you feel like you're ready to talk things over?"

Lucy clenched her jaw and put on the best defiant look she could muster. "Haven't I done enough? I told your killer what he wanted to know when he pulled me out of my bed the other night. What more do you expect?"

"What I expect is for you to show just a little more gratitude to the man who gave you a job when you were just about to start selling that pretty little body of yours to put food on your table. After all," he added while gesturing toward the window at his back, "you've seen for yourself what happens to those that don't show proper respect."

"That son of a bitch told me that this would clear things up between you and me," Lucy said desperately. "He said all I had to do was . . ." She paused just then as she thought about what she'd done.

THIRTY-NINE

The night before, after she and Clint had made love and fallen asleep in each other's arms, Lucy had awakened to see a face glaring through her window. It would have seemed like a nightmare, if not for the fact that that face belonged to no devil and the terror she felt was too real to come from any dream.

That face had belonged to a killer named Paul who was one of the men charged with enforcing Bittermeyer's every word. He'd stared through the glass, willing her to look at him, as though he'd been waiting there for hours for just that particular occasion.

Before she went out to see him, Lucy was tempted to wake Clint. After all, a man like him might have been able to do something against a killer like Paul. But there was also the thought that if Clint made the slightest mistake, then both he and Lucy would die in a hail of gunfire. The thought that brought Lucy outside in the end was that she would be dead the moment she even looked the wrong way at the man sharing her bed.

The deal had been simple.

Talk to everyone she knew in the area and tell Paul about any stranger she heard about in town. In fact, Lucy began to realize that Paul didn't even know that the man he was after was the same one sleeping in her bed. Her first intention then had been to get Paul to leave and then get Clint out as soon as possible.

"Hey," Paul whispered. His eyes darted toward Lucy's window as though he could plainly read the thoughts running through her mind. "Who's that inside there? Some new friend of yours or just someone with enough money to climb beneath your skirt?"

"He's nobody," she replied while fighting back a tremor that was creeping into her voice. "Nobody you would know, anyway."

Paul stepped up to the window and peered inside. After studying the bedroom for a few more seconds than he should have, he slowly turned to look at Lucy. "I don't recognize him. What's his name?"

"I'll do what you want. Just get away from my home and tell Bittermeyer that—"

"I've never seen him before. That makes him a stranger. You were working tonight when those boys were gunned down outside of the Rosewood, weren't you?"

Lucy swallowed once and nodded.

"And now," Paul continued, "you show up with a stranger in your bed after the stranger I'm looking for goes missing. Isn't that peculiar?"

"I swear I don't know what you're trying to say."

Paul's arm was a blur of motion. The only sound Lucy could hear was the rustle of the other man's shirt and the metallic click of a pistol's hammer being snapped into place. The only thing she could feel was the cold touch of a gun barrel beneath her chin.

Paul leaned in close enough that his breaths caused the red strands of hair hanging in front of Lucy's face to quiver with every one of his exhales. "I'll only ask this once, and if I don't believe your answer, your head's gonna be emptied out all over this wall. If I think you're telling the truth, I'll see to it that whatever debts you have with Bittermeyer . . . and we all got debts with him . . . they'll be wiped clean. Understand?"

Lucy tried to nod, but was unable to get herself to move. It was all she could do to get herself to breathe.

"Who's that man in your bedroom?" Paul asked.

Lucy's mind raced with so many possible lies she could feed to the killer. She tried to think of something that she could say convincingly enough to save both her and Clint's lives.

But the longer she thought, the more seconds passed by.

And when enough seconds had passed by, the gun barrel dug up a little deeper beneath her chin.

"I don't need you," Paul whispered. "I can go ask him myself . . . after I blow out the back of your fucking skull."

"His name's Clint," Lucy spat out before she could control herself. Tears welled up in the corners of her eyes and streamed down her face the moment she realized what she'd done. "He's the stranger you were asking about."

At that moment, Lucy could feel the pistol shifting against her jaw. There was another click within the weapon's mechanism and, for a second, she thought the hammer was on its way down toward the back of the bullet that would end her life.

But there was no shot. There was only Paul's voice.

"Good girl," he said while releasing the hammer and holstering his gun. "Now go back and get some more sleep. We'll be back for your stranger soon enough."

When Lucy felt the gun barrel move away from her skin, she closed her eyes and forced a welcome breath into her lungs. When she opened her eyes again, Paul was gone, his last words ringing ominously through her mind.

She wanted to tell Clint about what had happened.

She wanted to tell him to leave . . . just ride away from Random and never come back.

But somehow, her body wouldn't let her go back inside. There was something that made it impossible for her to even look through the window at the man whose life she'd just given away to save her own.

They would be back soon enough.

That notion swirled amid her thoughts, gathering force like a twister winding itself up into a full-blown tornado. Paul and the rest of Bittermeyer's killers would be back, and they wouldn't want to do anything but shoot down anyone in their path.

She knew this to be true.

She'd seen what happened to those that stood in Bittermeyer's way. People like that were buried somewhere in the ground outside of town, their graves marked only by the memories of those who'd dug them.

Lucy realized then that her words to Paul had only delayed what could happen to her. That same gun could be placed in the same spot beneath her chin, except at that time the outcome would be much different.

Thinking this, Lucy felt the tears start to flow and her heart begin to pound. Her entire body was shaking with fits of panic, and before she realized what she was doing, she'd already started running.

She didn't know where she was going exactly. All she wanted was to get away.

At the time, that had been enough.

FORTY

"He said all I had to do was tell him the truth," Lucy said once the recent memories had faded enough for her to concentrate on the present. "And I did."

"You most certainly did," Bittermeyer said. "And I'm not asking for anything else. Well . . . not much of anything, to be sure."

Lowering her head, Lucy knew that she'd only dug herself in deeper with Bittermeyer. Before, she'd only owed the man some money and her job, both of which could have been replaced. But now the lean boss of Random looked at her with a gleam in his brown eyes. He looked at her as though he was watching his own talons sink deeper into her flesh.

Lucy knew she'd already sentenced one man to death just by pointing her finger at him, but that still wasn't enough for Bittermeyer. It was enough for her, though. It was enough to make her feel like a killer herself.

"Don't worry," he said condescendingly. "I don't want you to do anything that you haven't done before. You just need to step outside and catch that stranger's eye. What did you say his name was? Clint, I believe? Yes . . . catch his eye and bring him to me. I'll let you know when."

Lucy didn't have to ask what would come after that. In fact, she could already hear the shot that would come once Clint was distracted. And she could see the look on his face when he stared at her for the last time.

"What's the matter, my dear?" Bittermeyer asked. "You look like you've lost your best friend. Are you more attached to this man than I know?"

Shaking her head, Lucy glanced over her shoulder at Stanton and then back to Bittermeyer. "No. I'm just . . . not used to this sort of thing."

"But you'll help me?"

"Yes," she said with a resigned nod. "I'll help you. It doesn't look like I have much choice in the matter anyway."

Bittermeyer reached to a box of cigars on top of his desk, pulled one out and ran it beneath his nose. After snipping off one end with a silver-plated cutter, he said, "No. It doesn't look that way at all."

With a nod from his boss, Stanton pulled Lucy to her feet and showed her out the door. He handed her off to some of the men posted outside and then stepped back into the office, shutting the door behind him.

"So what do you think?" Bittermeyer asked. "Is she really going to help us?"

"She looked awful scared, sir, but I don't suppose that matters much."

Bittermeyer nodded crisply. "Precisely. In fact, the more scared she is, the more attention she's likely to draw. And in a gunfight, every distraction you can call up in your favor is worth its weight in gold."

Settling into his thickly padded chair, Bittermeyer stroked his goatee and fished a match from his shirt pocket. "You've come a long way, Stanton. I daresay that seeing what happened to your dim-witted friends was just the thing you needed to bring you farther in my company."

Stanton recalled his "dim-witted friends" being cut down by the gun in the stranger's lightning-fast hand. Ever since then, he'd been thinking of things in a different way. Even Bittermeyer had been treating him like a different person. "I suppose so," he said.

"In fact, I'd like you to work with Connor and Paul in sweeping up the mess that the other boys started."

"You mean the fire, sir?"

"That was a means to an end. As much as I'd hoped one of those boys would get a lucky shot in, I didn't get my hopes up too high," Bittermeyer said as he struck a match and touched the little flame to the end of his cigar. "They were supposed to send my message and tire that stranger out." A smile formed across his face when he added, "I caught sight of him lugging barrels and stomping out flames just a minute or so ago and he couldn't have looked more ready to fall over.

"He may be fast, but he's only human. By the time Connor and Paul find him, he'll hardly be strong enough to lift his gun. And that," he said while puffing his cigar until the end was glowing red, "is where you come in, Stanton. You be sure that that redheaded bitch does what she's supposed to and doesn't try to warn that stranger what's coming his way. After that, just be sure to add your gun to the others when they blow that man straight to hell."

"I'll do my best, sir."

"No, Stanton. You'll do it . . . plain and simple. You'll do it or I'll have to assume that you're no better than the rest of those ingrates that think they can stab me in the back as much as it pleases them."

Stanton nodded grimly as he realized just how much was being set in front of him. Judging not so much by what Bittermeyer said, but by the way he said it, Stanton was being faced with a do-or-die proposition. He could either fulfill his duties or wind up like all the others that had been given similar choices.

Stanton knew damn well what happened to them. He still had some of the dirt from their graves beneath his fingernails.

Once Bittermeyer got up and stared intently out the window, Stanton knew he'd been dismissed. In a way, he was glad to be out of that office, and stepping back into the saloon proper was a welcome return to his old life.

It used to be that he would spend his hours at that bar talking to Bittermeyer and his friends like a group of regular men who enjoyed each other's company. Sure, there had always been the rumors of what a monster Bittermeyer was. There had even been things he'd seen with his own eyes to show Stanton what kind of man made the decisions in this town. But through all that, Stanton figured he could just sit back and reap the rewards of being on Bittermeyer's good side.

After all, the town ran smoothly, didn't it? Random was full of nice homes and prosperous businesses.

Only now did Stanton see the foundation that lay beneath Random's soil. Only now did he realize all the blood that had been spilt to keep the town within Bittermeyer's grasp.

And just when he thought his world couldn't become any darker, Stanton realized it was about to get much, much worse.

FORTY-ONE

The front door of the Rosewood flew open to slam violently against the wall before swinging back into place. Catching it as he stepped inside, Paul scanned the saloon with fiery eyes and focused immediately on Stanton.

"You," he said while jabbing a finger in the air. "Come with us."

Just then, Paul stepped aside to reveal Connor's slender, coiled frame taking up the doorway. Seeing one of these killers was enough to send chills down the spine of anyone who knew the men. Seeing them both together was like staring into the face of the grim reaper himself.

"What are you waiting for?" Connor rasped in his permanently scratchy voice. "Get the lead out of your ass before I come over there and put my boot in it."

Stanton moved as though some invisible hand was tugging him along. As much as he wanted to run the opposite way, he simply couldn't dredge up the strength necessary to defy the hired killers. And so, before he knew what was going on, Stanton found himself walking out the door . . . and staring straight into the face of the stranger who'd put all of this into motion.

• • •

Clint could still feel the fire burning inside of him, as though his guts had been put to the torch along with all of the houses in the Rosewood's back lot. He knew that Bittermeyer's eyes would be on him the moment he started walking toward the saloon. And he also knew that there would most likely be more gunmen coming to meet him.

He knew all of that, but he simply couldn't bring himself to care. Too much had happened in Random. And if none of the locals could do anything about it, that meant the job fell to someone who could. It was a burden Clint was only too used to carrying.

Since all of the townspeople were hurrying to lend a hand with the fires, Clint didn't attract much attention as he walked to the front of the saloon. The locals that rushed by him only glanced at him long enough to dodge him as they ran by, before looking back to the smoking homes farther down the street.

When Clint stood in front of the Rosewood just as Connor and Paul stepped outside—that was when some of the folks nearby stopped what they were doing and took full notice.

For the next few seconds, Clint stood as though he'd been chiseled from stone and placed in that spot. The only thing to move was his eyes, which shifted slowly between Connor and Paul. He noticed that Stanton was there as well, but he instinctively knew that the third man wasn't much of a threat.

"What's the matter, stranger?" Connor rasped. "Did you get tired from lugging all them buckets?"

Paul nodded slightly. "Nah. I'd say he was stopping by to say good-bye or get a quick drink on his way out of town. That sound about right?"

Clint listened to what the men said, but reacted about as much as the statue he resembled. The expression on his face didn't shift in the slightest, and not even the first hint of emotion showed in his eyes.

Observing this as the smirk melted away from his face, Connor stepped forward and raised an empty hand. With deliberate slowness, he curled his fingers up and down in a mocking wave. "If you're gonna leave, then go right on ahead. Be sure to come back next time you feel the urge to see another bonfire."

But Clint didn't move.

Now Paul stepped forward. He walked down the steps leading from the boardwalk to the street and stopped as soon as his boots touched the spongy mud. "Mr. Bittermeyer has a bone to pick with you. He says you need to pay for what you done to his men. He told my friend and me to take that payment from you. You had the chance to make your payment without a fight, but that's long gone. Now you're gonna have to take it the hard way." His hand dropped down to the double rig around his waist, palms resting against the handles of twin .45 pistols.

Before Paul's skin touched the guns, Clint had already drawn the modified Colt and aimed it at him.

"You've got it wrong," Clint said. "Bittermeyer's the one who needs to pay for what he's done. Not only to me, but to all of these people. I'm taking him to the law, no matter how far I have to ride to get there."

"Well, we can't allow that," Connor said, his voice dripping with venom.

Clint looked between the two men, sizing them up in the space of a heartbeat. Although Paul still stood with his hands on his guns, Connor had yet to even make a move to arm himself. Since he had yet to see either one of them in action, Clint still had to consider them both as wild cards.

Suddenly Clint caught sight of something out of the corner of his eye. What he saw was a group of people gathered near the side of the saloon. Some of them still had buckets in their hands, but they had obviously been distracted by the brewing hostilities in front of the Rosewood before they'd lent their services to putting out the nearby fire.

Seeing the expanding audience he was attracting, Clint knew that one of them might get hurt if the lead started to fly. Besides, the fires were dying down and required every drop of water that could be found to put them out completely.

"Tell you what," Clint said after considering his options. "If you want to punish me so badly, then you can just come and do it yourselves. I'm tired of looking at this eyesore of a saloon."

And without another word of explanation, Clint started walking backward toward the alley across from the Rosewood. He was ready for either of the gunmen to make his move, but didn't expect either one to do so just yet.

Sure enough, as Clint entered the alley, both Connor and Paul started walking toward him. Wry grins adorned both of the killers' faces, and they couldn't have appeared any happier to follow their target into what was surely their most familiar territory.

The only thing that put Clint's mind to rest was the sound of rushing footsteps and raised voices as the locals who'd been gathered to watch a fight suddenly remembered that they still had a fire to put out. Unfortunately, that was exactly where the good news left off and the bad news picked up.

Clint was well into the alley by now and watched as Paul walked straight toward him. The more slender Connor ran quickly for the mouth of the alley as well, but turned sharply and disappeared from Clint's view. Stanton was coming forward also, but was doing his best to keep Paul between himself and Clint.

Every step Clint took echoed like cannon fire within the tight confines of the alley. Paul's steps became increasingly louder as well the closer he got to the narrow, wooden canyon. The buildings were close enough together that Clint wouldn't have been able to stretch out both arms without touching both hands against the sides of the alley.

Soon, another set of footsteps grew louder in his ears, amplified by the tight space. Clint took a quick glance toward the end of the alley, to find Connor running into view after having dashed around the building to cut him off.

"Looks like you got nowhere left to go," Paul said.

Connor's breath was racing, which made his voice even more scratchy when he said, "That ain't true. He's got somewhere to go. About six feet under."

FORTY-TWO

Clint knew he only had a matter of seconds before he would be caught in the middle of a crossfire. And since the men on either side of his alley were more than likely professional gunslingers, a crossfire was the last place Clint wanted to be.

He knew he'd wanted to get away from anyplace that innocent bystanders might get hurt, but he hadn't had too many options. Now, looking at the direction he'd decided to take, Clint wondered if it wouldn't have been better to think things through a little more before setting off. But he'd made his choice and now was not the time to question it.

All he needed to do now was think of a way to live through it.

Paul and Connor began walking into the alley, taking their sweet time since they knew they had Clint right where they wanted him. Their hands rested on the handles of their guns as they closed in even further. The tension between the three men was strong enough to crackle like lightning between charged clouds.

Turning his back to the wall, Clint moved so he could keep both of the other men at least in the outskirts of his vision. As far as he could tell, Stanton had yet to come into the alley. And though the fourth man could have been setting himself into position on one of the rooftops or even directly behind Paul, Stanton was still the least of Clint's worries.

Clint's back smacked against the building behind him. Taking a quick glance, he saw a small, hastily painted sign hanging next to a narrow door. It read: "Winslow's Photography Studio." Reaching out with his left hand, Clint felt for the door's handle just as Paul started removing his .45s from their holster.

Connor was reaching for something as well, but although he carried a pistol in one hand, his other was wrapped around a piece of sharpened steel longer than his own forearm. Both men seemed to be enjoying themselves as they prepared their weapons and moved in for the kill.

Clint was still trying to find a door handle and soon realized that there wasn't one. Pressing his back against the door, he lifted his right knee and swung back with his boot in a kick that had all of his strength behind it.

The door resisted the kick for one split second that seemed like an eternity inside Clint's mind, but the flimsy wood and simple latch were no match against the force of Clint's blow, and the door was soon exploding inward as if it had been dynamited from its hinges.

Both Connor and Paul noticed the instant the door broke loose. Their eyes narrowed and every bit of hesitation drained from their minds and bodies as they drew their weapons and surged forward.

The crackle of gunfire blasted through the alley, sending bullets that chewed into the door frame and blasted holes through the wall where Clint had just been standing.

Launching himself backward through space, Clint reflexively slapped the Colt back into its holster so he could have both hands free to break his fall and wouldn't have to worry about dropping the gun. As soon as he heard the shots coming from outside and saw where the bullets were landing, he knew he'd made a smart decision in picking a different spot to make his stand.

As he thought this, his backside made contact with the floor of the studio. Clint let the momentum flow through his body, pushing off with his feet while rolling onto his shoulders and the back of his head. Although it wasn't the prettiest move in the world, he managed to land roughly on his knees and facing the shattered door.

The first one to step into his sight was Paul, who swung into the doorway with both .45s blazing.

His first two shots upon stepping into the studio were aimed to blow the head off any man standing in his path. Since Clint wasn't standing, the rounds went high, taking a chunk out of an expensive-looking frame and shattering a window.

Keeping his head down while hopping to his feet, Clint drew the Colt and fired in one swift motion, taking a piece of flesh out of Paul just below his ribs. The gunman snarled in pain and staggered to one side, allowing Connor to enter the room from directly behind him.

The sheer speed with which Connor moved took Clint by surprise. Not only was the killer pouncing at him like a crazed wildcat, but he was charging in with the blade at the ready, his pistol all but forgotten in his other hand.

Clint's first reaction was to take a shot at Connor before he was in the machete's range. Aiming more out of reflex than sight, he shifted the Colt and pulled its trigger while also trying to get his legs more stable beneath him.

Connor's shoulder popped as though a bubble had been beneath his skin, spraying out a fine mist of blood as Clint's bullet passed through flesh and bone. If he felt the injury at all, Connor didn't show it as he lowered his shoulder into the charge and raised the wicked-looking machete over his head.

A primal howl came from Connor's throat. Slamming his shoulder into Clint's midsection, he shoved his target back a few steps and sent the machete streaking through the air toward Clint's neck.

The smaller man impacted against Clint like a boxcar, and it was all he could do to stay on his feet while the breath was forced from his lungs. Before he could even think about sucking down some air, he saw the glint of steel to his left and raised his hand reflexively to block whatever was coming.

Connor's wrist slammed against Clint's forearm hard enough to send sparks of pain to both men's shoulders. The machete's blade came slicing down toward its target, but stopped less than an inch short.

Staring up at the oiled blade, Clint could see every chip along the machete's edge and could even smell the sharpened steel as it was pressed down toward his cheek. Turning his attention to Connor, Clint pulled some air into his aching lungs and strained all his muscles to their limit, which was just enough to push Connor away from him.

Even as he stumbled back, Connor took a wild swing with his blade and spat a curse toward his prey.

Clint ducked beneath the incoming machete and delivered a vicious uppercut into Connor's gut. The blow doubled the other man over just in time to accept the Colt's handle which came crashing down on the back of his neck.

Running on pure instinct, Clint moved to one side before Connor fell to the floor, knowing full well that Paul wouldn't wait to start firing once his partner was out of the way. Sure enough, the air was immediately filled with lead. Thunder roared within the studio and was soon joined by the sound of breaking glass and toppling furniture.

Already struggling to his feet, Connor lifted his head and let out another animalistic snarl while charging forward once again. This time, however, he was preparing to fire the pistol in his hand as well as taking another swing with the machete.

Clint felt as though he was riding on the crest of a tidal wave, his body moving less than a foot ahead of the bullets which were tracking ever closer toward him. He knew that one of those .45s would find their mark and quickly adjusted his aim to tip the odds more toward his favor.

As he brought up the Colt, Clint felt like the pistol was melding into his hand, to become part of his own body. He didn't think about sighting down the barrel or even pulling the trigger. All he thought about was where he wanted the bullet to go, and amid a blast of smoke, it was there.

There was the sharp clang of metal on metal as the gun in Paul's left hand was struck by Clint's bullet. The impact jerked his hand toward Connor while also forcing Paul to reflexively pull the trigger.

Paul's misguided shot whipped through the air over Connor's head, causing the feral killer to drop to the floor in midcharge. The fight was only set off course for a second, but Clint was ready to take full advantage of it and his Colt was already pointed in the right direction.

No more retreat, Clint thought as the battle turned in his favor.

FORTY-THREE

All it took was the slightest turn of Clint's wrist to aim at a spot directly between Paul's eyes. One squeeze of the trigger, and the tall gunman was reeling back through the broken door, his crossed eyes staring up in disbelief at the freshly drilled hole in his forehead.

Connor didn't miss a beat as he regained his balance and brought up his pistol. He was still snarling as he pulled the trigger.

Outguessing Connor by no more than half a second, Clint spun to his left and dropped to one knee. The motion barely put him out of harm's way as Connor's bullet hissed through the air to his right.

Rather than snap back the hammer for another shot, Connor tossed the pistol to the floor and ran toward Clint with the machete gripped in both hands.

Even though Clint knew better than to underestimate the other man's speed a second time, he was still taken by surprise as rage and desperation pushed Connor's prowess to even greater lengths. The smaller man charged toward him as though he had a steam engine pushing him on a collision course to his waiting target. Before Clint could squeeze off another shot, Connor was already on him.

The Colt barked again, but delivered its round into the ceiling. Clint wondered how he'd let that happen, but was immediately answered by a burning pain in his collarbone. As soon as he felt the pain, he saw the handle of the machete right next to his eye, the blade digging deeply into his flesh just an inch shy of his neck.

"I got ya, you son of a bitch," Connor rasped. "And now I'm gonna butcher you like a side of beef."

As he spoke, Connor leaned on the machete to drive it further down into the bone. He smiled with a crazed look in his eye, his face reflecting less emotion than the dead wood and steel in his grasp.

Clint's jaw locked against the agony that burned through his upper body. The sound of metal scraping against bone echoed loud enough inside his skull to block out everything else. The noise rattled Clint's mind and caused his teeth to clamp even closer together.

A hot trail of blood started pouring down his back and chest like lava streaming from the lip of a volcano. And just when he thought he might pass out from the pain, Clint felt his entire body being pulled to one side and then tossed to the other as Connor began prying his machete from where it had been lodged.

Already, Clint could feel his strength draining out of him and spilling from the wound onto his collar. He knew he was going to be in much more danger if his vision started to fade as well, since that would mean that he was probably bleeding out.

But the pain was keeping him awake and he was fairly certain that the machete hadn't cut anything too major. That would have to be decided later, however, since Connor seemed intent on hacking Clint's head clean off his shoulders.

Connor grunted and got ready to pull the machete away. His face twisted into a gruesome mask as he readied himself for one more attempt to move back with his weapon in hand.

At that moment, Clint felt his consciousness start to waver as another wave of pain surged through his body. As much as he wanted to get the machete out of his shoulder, he saw one more chance available to him before loss of blood and agonizing pain threatened to tip the scales back into Connor's favor.

Mustering up every last bit of strength, Clint reached up with his left hand and grabbed hold of the machete just as Connor tried to pull it free. Clint managed to hold on just tight enough to keep the blade lodged in place, despite the fact that the edge of the weapon dug deeply into his fingers.

The look on Connor's face turned from savage victory to surprise as his entire body came to a sudden stop. He hadn't been expecting the machete to stay put, and when it did, Connor nearly stumbled backward due to misplaced footing.

Looking toward Clint for an explanation of what had thrown him off balance, Connor turned to stare directly down the barrel of a modified Colt. His world exploded in a sudden blast of sound and smoke as his life was emptied into the air behind his head.

Connor stood there for a second, staring disbelievingly into oblivion. Finally, after a few inarticulate grunts, he dropped to his knees and then fell over onto his side.

After he was certain neither gunmen was going to get up, Clint lowered himself to the floor and rested his back against a large wooden cabinet. He was careful to lean forward so no part of the machete in his shoulder was nudged even by accident.

Clint dropped his gun and clenched his eyes shut while taking a deep breath. With one hand around the machete's handle and the other on the back of the blade, he pushed the air out of his lungs and tore the machete from his shoulder.

The length of sharpened steel came out of his bone and slid through severed meat for what seemed like a year and a half before it was finally free of his body. A stifled scream came from Clint's throat without him even knowing it was there. To him, it seemed as though the room was filled with the cries of a wounded animal, and when the machete clanged to the floor, the sound died away.

Reaching up to feel his shoulder, Clint shook the encroaching cobwebs from his brain and spotted a figure standing in the shattered doorway. His instincts told him to go for his gun, but Clint's body wasn't so quick to answer the call.

Then, Clint took a closer look at the figure.

It was Stanton. And judging by the look of stunned terror on his face, he'd seen everything that had just happened, including Clint tearing the machete from his own body. All the color drained from Stanton's face as he turned and ran down the alley as fast as his legs could carry him.

Despite everything that had happened and the pain that tore through every one of his nerves, Clint couldn't help but laugh.

FORTY-FOUR

The town of Random might not have had any law, but Clint sure hoped that it had a doctor. After getting a chance to catch his breath, he tore pieces from his shirt and pressed the material against the gaping wound in his shoulder.

The pain started to die down as soon as the machete had been removed, and within seconds, Clint heard another set of footsteps coming toward the door. This time, however, the steps were lighter than before, scampering up the few stairs leading from the alley like the approach of a frightened mouse.

Clint held his Colt at the ready, but lowered it immediately when he saw Lucy's red hair come into view.

"Oh, dear Lord," she said. Ignoring the gun, she rushed toward him and dropped down to his side. "The whole town is talking about what happened and I had to come see for myself. Are you all right?"

"I don't know," Clint said as he moved the makeshift bandage from his shoulder. "You tell me."

Rather than turn away from the grisly sight, Lucy leaned in closer and carefully took the strips of material from Clint's hands. "It's not bleeding too badly. I'd say you got awful lucky."

Clint grunted as he shifted his weight. "Funny, but I don't feel too lucky."

"Well, one of my brothers nearly got his arm cut off on the farm back home. The doc had to take it off before the day was out and I'll never forget the sight." Pressing her fingers as delicately as she could on and around his wound, she said, "This looks like you got hit on mostly bone. I can see where the blade went in and it's a pretty clean cut."

Listening to her speak, Clint tested Lucy's theory by trying to move his arm and flex his fingers. Although the pain was great, he didn't have too much trouble in either task. After Lucy had cleaned it up a bit using strips from the bottom edge of her dress, he felt the wound once again and was surprised to find that it really wasn't even that wide. Just a thin, deep gouge on the front part of his shoulder. He could feel the bigger muscles and tendons moving slightly farther back and realized he'd been damn lucky, indeed.

"Never thought I'd be thankful to get hit with such a sharp blade," Clint said while shaking his head.

Lucy fussed some more with the dressing. "That's one of the things that kept the wound so neat. But I wouldn't take too much time to thank your lucky stars if I were you."

"Why not?"

"Because I saw Mr. Bittermeyer standing in front of his saloon when I ran over here. He seemed to be waiting for his men to come back, and when they don't . . . well . . . let's just say he didn't look too happy."

Clint struggled to get to his feet and then bent down to retrieve his Colt. Emptying the pistol with one hand, he kept his left arm as motionless as possible. "If he wasn't happy then, I can guarantee you he won't be any happier in a few minutes."

"Why?" Lucy asked in a voice that was suddenly filled with panic. "Are you going back out there? You can't. I won't let you!"

Placing the Colt in his left hand, Clint found that he was able to grab the pistol just fine as he slid fresh cartridges into the cylinder. "You know as well as I that if I don't go out there, he'll be coming in here. And the only thing I've got going for me in this condition is staying one step ahead of him. Besides, you know that things will only get worse around here unless something is done about Bittermeyer. If he gets away with everything he's done plus this as well, he'll figure nothing can stop him and he can burn down as many homes as he wants. More hired guns aren't that hard to find."

Lucy listened to him and started to protest several times, but stopped herself before the words came out. Finally, she nodded solemnly and slid her arms around Clint's waist. "I know all that, Clint. It's just that I wish someone besides you could take the risk. You've gone through so much already."

"Which is exactly why I've got to finish this. I don't know how Bittermeyer got his hooks into this town or how he kept them there for so long, but I do know that he needs to be taken out of this town for good. I can't just ride out of here knowing that I've left a monster in charge."

"But it's not even your town," Lucy said in disbelief. "You've only been here for two days."

"I'm not the one who started this," Clint replied. "But if I have to, I'll be the one to finish it." With that, he snapped the Colt shut and dropped it into his holster.

Lucy quickly tore off some more strips of material and tied them around Clint's wound as best as she could. Already, the flow of blood was tapering off, and it seemed to be mostly absorbed by the hastily created dressing. After tying it off, she slid her hands through Clint's hair and pulled him closer. "When this is over," she whispered, "I'll owe you one hell of a thank-you."

Clint savored the touch of her lips against his skin and the smell of her wispy, scarlet hair. "Yes," he said. "You sure will."

Stepping back, Lucy resisted the urge to throw herself in front of the door or try to hold Clint back any way she could. Instead, she watched him walk out of the studio and step into the alley.

Clint was ready for anything as he walked outside. The first thing he did was look to either side, preparing himself to be rushed by another wave of Bittermeyer's men. But there was nothing to greet him as he emerged from the smoky studio—nothing but a cool breeze and the smell of burnt gunpowder.

Remembering what Lucy had told him about Bittermeyer waiting in front of the saloon, Clint walked toward the back of the alley instead of the way he'd come in. As he moved, he could feel the wound in his shoulder protesting with grating spikes of pain. They didn't seem as bad as before, however, which meant either that it really wasn't as bad as it could have been, or that he was just getting used to the throbbing agony.

Either way, Clint knew that he would be able to use the arm to some degree if he had to. And the fleeting fear of a doctor hacking into him with a saw had also passed. If he could move his arm at all, he wasn't about to let anybody take it from him.

Clint used those thoughts as a distraction to take his mind away from the lingering pain while he walked around the building next to the studio. He figured he was taking the same path Connor had taken to cut him off before and knew that it was only a matter of time before

Bittermeyer got tired of waiting for him in front of the Rosewood.

When he rounded the final corner, Clint got a look at the front of the huge saloon just as its owner was stepping into the middle of the street.

Bittermeyer walked as though he didn't have a care in the world. He stood facing the front of the alley, his hand drifting toward his shoulder holster and the silver-handled Smith & Wesson waiting there.

"If you're waiting for your men," Clint said, "you'll be standing there for a long time."

At the sound of Clint's voice, Bittermeyer spun toward the other side of the building he'd been watching. He knew better than to try and draw his pistol right away, but his hand stayed as close as he could manage without provoking a response. "You put on a hell of a show, mister. But I'm not about to roll over and let you take my town away from me."

"I don't want your town," Clint replied. "I just want you out of it."

FORTY-FIVE

Bittermeyer squared his shoulders and puffed out his chest like an animal that was about to mark its territory. "I'll tell you what. Since you got through all of my men, I've got a proposition for you. We can work side by side and build this town up into something even more profitable than it already is. What do you say?"

Clint's eyes locked onto Bittermeyer and didn't waver for so much as a moment. "You heard me the first time. You're not wanted here, so you've only got two choices. Get out."

"And what if I don't care for that choice?"

In response, Clint raised his chin defiantly and dropped his hand so that it was level with his Colt.

Nodding, Bittermeyer turned his body into the classic duelist's stance, with both shoulders in line with his opponent's to make himself a smaller target. "Do I at least get to know your name before I kill you?"

The question hung in the air for a second or two. Unanswered, it dissipated like so much smoke over a cooking fire, leaving both men staring across about ten yards of empty street.

Clint's body was pumped full of adrenaline and waiting for the slightest hint of movement from the other man. The pain in his shoulder was wiped away by the pounding of his heart and the rush of blood through his veins.

Bittermeyer was the picture of calm. His smug expression had dropped away to be replaced by a blank mask that mirrored Clint's own. He watched the man across from him and thought about what caliber of a fighter was required to come in and tear through all the men he'd thrown at him.

He knew this stranger was more than lucky. He was damn good. But Bittermeyer was confident in his own skills. In fact, the thought of losing never even crossed his mind.

Tension mixed with expectation, urging Clint to draw and get this fight over with before his wounds caught up to him. But in this calm before the storm, every movement was crucial, especially the first one.

Bittermeyer fought to keep his arms still and his feet from shifting. A bead of sweat pushed out from his brow and dripped into one eye, the salty sting almost causing him to flinch. Almost . . . but not quite.

Clint let out a slow breath, feeling the final second draw closer.

Bittermeyer inched toward his gun, the holster seeming to be so far away despite the fact that it was less than a few inches from his grasp.

Clint spotted the motion and prepared.

Bittermeyer steeled himself. His nerves started to twist in his gut and a hairline crack formed in his resolve.

The instant Bittermeyer went for his shoulder holster, Clint reacted. Not even thinking about his speed or motion, Clint let his reflexes take over in a quick blur of movement.

He barely had a chance to feel the Colt in his hand before Clint felt his finger close around the trigger. All the while, he hadn't taken his eyes from Bittermeyer and was watching as the other man cleared leather and pointed his Smith & Wesson right on target.

One shot cracked through the air, followed by another so closely that both sounds nearly blended into one.

Bittermeyer twitched once and took a step back, a victorious smile creeping onto his face. The mere fact that he was alive caused his heart to race and the air to drain from his lungs. "What?" he grunted as he felt his strength fading away. "But I . . ."

Keeping the other man in his sights, Clint almost fired again. That was when he saw the wet, crimson stain forming on Bittermeyer's chest.

"This can't be," Bittermeyer said quietly. Looking down at his gun, wondering why he couldn't seem to pull the trigger again, he saw all the color draining from the flesh of his hands.

Soon after, his vision started to go.

And one second later, Bittermeyer's world went black.

Clint stood over the body, not looking up until he knew that Bittermeyer was truly gone. When he holstered the Colt and glanced around him, he saw at least two dozen locals standing at the corner, their figures outlined by the smoke that poured in from the dying fires.

One of those figures stepped forward. She was almost unrecognizable beneath the soot and grime coating her face, but the blond hair still shone through.

"Hello, Belle," Clint said. "You still interested in owning the Rosewood?"

FORTY-SIX

The first thing Clint had wanted to do was saddle up Eclipse and ride away from Random. Of course, that had been three days ago and a lot had happened since then.

Everyone in the town was seeing to the reconstruction of the homes that had been torched and going about the first steps of putting together their own council to make the decisions that Bittermeyer had kept to himself.

Clint didn't have much interest in politics or who would work with the next deputy who was due to arrive any time now. He didn't even care about how Bittermeyer's interests were split up. He was too busy getting some much needed attention of his own from a certain redhead who was a firm believer in healthy bedside manner.

"That's looking much better," Lucy said while tending to the fresh bandages around Clint's shoulder.

Clint looked around the lush accommodations that were situated above the Rosewood. The floors were dark, polished wood and the furniture was made from carved mahogany. "I've planted myself on this bed for the last couple of days and I still don't want to leave."

"Who says you have to? It's about time for you to get some exercise, anyway."

"Doctor's orders?"

"No. Mine."

Lucy shrugged out of her dress and let the garment fall to the floor. She stood naked before Clint and ran her hands over her body, tracing the same path taken by Clint's eyes. By the time her fingers slid down the outside of her thighs, her nipples were hard little nubs at the ends of firm, rounded breasts.

Beneath the blanket, Clint was only wearing his britches, and when he pulled the cover away from him, he felt only the slightest twinge of pain from his shoulder. He overplayed the discomfort, which brought a sympathetic pout to Lucy's lips.

"Ohhh," she cooed. "Do you need me to help you feel better?"

She crawled over Clint and slowly undressed him, using her teeth to slide the britches down his legs. Her hands moved back up his body and came to rest over his stiff penis. As she lifted herself over him, Lucy couldn't wait to have Clint inside of her. She lowered herself down, taking him in between her legs as a satisfied moan slipped from her lips.

Clint took hold of her by the hips and guided her up and down, back and forth, their bodies grinding together in a slow, intense rhythm. All the while, Lucy arched her back, pressed her palms against his chest and rode him.

They made love all throughout the night and well into the next morning.

There were picnics and celebrations in Random, but as far as Clint was concerned, the town could get along just fine without him for a while.

Watch for

A MAN OF THE GUN

248th novel in the exciting GUNSMITH series
from Jove

Coming in August!

J.R. ROBERTS
THE GUNSMITH